"What am I going to do about you?"

Angeline asked aloud as she stepped forward again, right into the vee of his legs. Her chocolate-brown eyes were on a level with his mouth, and their focus seemed to be fixated there.

"You're going to bandage me up," he said, but his voice was gruff. Damn near hoarse.

"In a minute," Angeline whispered. She leaned into him, tilting her head and light as a whisper, she rubbed her lips over his.

She'd started out feeling tenderness.

That was all, Angeline reassured herself. Just tenderness for this man whose unexpected acts of kindness touched her just as much as his more "creative" stunts shocked her.

But tenderness was abruptly eaten up in the incendiary flames that rose far too rapidly for her to fight.

Instead, she stood there, caught, as wildfire seemed to lick through them both.

Dear Reader,

Many years ago, I wrote about a minor character—a little girl, orphaned in another country, who snagged the heart of one of the Clay brothers, Daniel. In the end, not only was Daniel united with his soul mate, Maggie, and her little blond munchkin, J.D., but their new family grew even more when they were joined by sweet Angeline.

Little did I know that some day Angeline would grow up and find a story of her own, or that the secret agency partly responsible for that long-ago rescue from the orphanage would play such a part of so many of my stories. From one agent to another, that Hollins-Winword world just seems to keep growing, ever entwining, and even I am sometimes surprised with the pairings that result.

But that's one of those fascinating—and often frustrating!—things about writing…you think you know what your characters are going to do, and who they'll end up with, but quite often they have an entirely different idea. I never really intended Angeline for Brody Paine, but once he stuck his handsome nose in her business, well…this author had to just move out of the way and let them both have their way.

After all. Who wants to stand in the way of true love?

Allison

WED IN WYOMING

ALLISON LEIGH

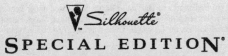

SPECIAL EDITION

Published by Silhouette Books

America's Publisher of Contemporary Romance

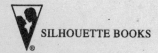

SILHOUETTE BOOKS

ISBN-13: 978-0-373-28081-0
ISBN-10:   0-373-28081-5

WED IN WYOMING

Copyright © 2007 by Allison Lee Davidson

Visit Silhouette Books at www.eHarlequin.com

Printed in U.S.A.

ALLISON LEIGH

started early by writing a Halloween play that her grade-school class performed. Since then, though her tastes have changed, her love for reading has not. And her writing appetite simply grows more voracious by the day.

She has been a finalist in the RITA® Award and Holt Medallion contests. But the true highlights of her day as a writer are when she receives word from a reader that she laughed, cried or lost a night of sleep while reading one of her books.

Born in Southern California, Allison has lived in several cities in four different states. She has been, at one time or another, a cosmetologist, a computer programmer and a secretary. She has recently begun writing full-time after spending nearly a decade as an administrative assistant for a busy neighborhood church, and she currently makes her home in Arizona with her family. She loves to hear from her readers, who can write to her at P.O. Box 40772, Mesa, AZ 85274-0772.

For my editor, Ann Leslie. Thank you for your patience, flexibility and general excellence. I think we've come a long way together!

Prologue

November

"**A**re you insane? What if someone sees you here?" Angeline Clay looked away from the tall man standing in the shadows of the big house to the wedding reception guests milling around behind her, barely twenty yards away.

"They won't." The man's deep voice was amused. "You forget, sweet cheeks, what I *do* for a living."

She rolled her eyes. They stood outside the

circle of pretty lights that had been strung around the enormous awning protecting the tables and the dance floor from the chilly Wyoming weather. Her cousin Leandra and her brand-new husband, Evan Taggart, were in the center of the floor dancing away, surrounded by nearly every other member of Angeline's extensive family. "I'm not likely to forget, Brody," she assured drily.

Since then, her brief encounters with the man had been few and far between, but they'd nevertheless been memorable.

Annoying, really, considering that Angeline prided herself on keeping her focus squarely where it belonged. Which was most assuredly *not* the impossible appeal of the elusive Brody Paine.

She flexed her bare fingers around the empty platter that she had been on her way to the kitchen to refill when Brody had stepped into her path. "How'd you even know I was here, anyway?"

The corner of his lips lifted. "It's a small world, babe. You know that."

Sweet cheeks. Babe.

She stifled a sigh. She couldn't recall Brody *ever* using her actual name. Which was probably one of the reasons why she'd never tried very hard to take the man seriously when it came to anything of a personal nature.

When it came to the work he did, however, she took him quite seriously because Brody Paine was well and truly one of the good guys. Since she'd learned at a particularly early age that the world was definitely on the shy side when it came to such people, she tried to give credit where it was due.

"I'm just visiting Weaver," she reminded him. "For the Thanksgiving holiday and Leandra's wedding. I'm going back to Atlanta soon."

He blandly reeled off her flight number, telling her not very subtly that he was perfectly aware of her schedule. "The agency likes to keep track of its assets."

She looked behind her again, but there was nobody within earshot. Of course. Brody wouldn't be likely to mention the agency if there had been. "I'm hardly an asset," she reminded him needlessly. She was a courier of sorts, true. But in the five years she'd worked for the agency, all she conveyed were pieces of information from one source to another. Even then, she was called on to do so only once or twice a year. It was a schedule that seemed to suit everyone.

"Believe me, hon. You've got more than any woman's fair share of assets," he assured drily. His gaze—she'd never been certain if it was naturally blue or brown because she'd seen his eye color differ over the years— traveled down her body. "Of course for some stubborn reason you keep refusing to share them with *me*."

She'd seen appreciation in men's eyes when they looked at her since she'd hit puberty. She was used to it. But she still felt absurdly grateful for the folds of the cashmere cape that flowed around her taupe-colored dress beneath it. "That's right," she said dismissively. "I assume this *isn't* a social call?"

His lips twitched again. "Only because you're a stubborn case, sweet cheeks."

Her lips tightened. "Brody—"

"Don't get your panties in a twist." He lifted one long-fingered hand. "I'm actually in the middle of another gig." He looked amused again. "But I was asked to give you this."

She realized that a small piece of paper was tucked between his index and middle finger. She plucked it free, careful not to touch him, only to nearly jump out of her skin when his fingers suddenly closed around her wrist.

She gave him a startled look.

The amusement from his face had been wiped away. "This is important."

Nerves tightened her throat. She wasn't used to seeing Brody looking so serious. "Isn't it always?" He'd told her, chapter and verse, from the very beginning just how important and sensitive her work with Hollins-Winword was.

"Like everything else in life, importance can be relative."

Behind them, the deejay was calling for everyone's attention since the bride and groom were preparing to cut their wedding cake. "I need to get back there. Before someone comes looking for me."

He slowly released her wrist. She stopped herself from rubbing the tingling that remained there just in time.

The man was entirely too observant. Which was, undoubtedly, one of the qualities that made him such an excellent agent. But the last thing she wanted him to know was that he had *any* kind of affect on her.

They were occasionally connected business associates and that was all. If the guy knew she'd been infatuated with him for years—well, she simply didn't want him knowing. Period. Maybe the knowledge would make a difference to him, and maybe it wouldn't. But she didn't intend to find out.

Playing immune to him was already hard enough.

She couldn't imagine how hard it would be if she spent any real time with the man.

He gave that small smile of his that had her wondering if mind reading was among his bag of tricks. "See you next time, babe." He lifted his chin in the direction of the partygoers. "Drink some champagne for me."

She glanced back, too. Leandra and Evan were standing in front of the enormous, tiered wedding cake. "I can probably get you a glass without anyone noticing. Cake, too."

She looked back when he didn't answer.

The only thing she saw was the dark, tall form of him disappearing into the cold night.

Chapter One

May

"I still think you're insane."

Since Angeline had last seen Brody Paine almost six months ago, he'd grown a scruffy brown beard that didn't quite mask the smile he gave at her pronouncement.

His sandy-brown hair hung thick and long around his ears, clearly in desperate need of a cut, and along with that beard, he looked vaguely piratical.

"Seems like you're always telling me that, babe."

Angeline lifted her eyebrows pointedly. They were sitting in a Jeep that was currently stuck lug nut deep in Venezuelan mud. "Take a clue from the theme," she suggested, raising her voice to be heard above the pounding rain.

As usual, he seemed to pay no heed of her opinion. Instead, he peered through the rain-washed windshield, drumming his thumb on the steering wheel. The vehicle itself looked as if it had been around about a half century.

It no longer possessed such luxuries as doors, and the wind that had been carrying sheets of rain for each of the three days since Angeline had arrived in Venezuela kept up its momentum, throwing a stinging spray across her and Brody.

The enormous weather system that was supposed to have veered away from land and calmly die out over the middle of the ocean hadn't behaved that way at all. Instead, it had squatted over them like some tormenting toad, bringing with it this incessant rain and wind. May might be too early for a hurricane, but Mother Nature didn't seem to care much for the official calendar.

She huddled deeper in the seat. The hood of her khaki-colored rain poncho hid most of her head, but she still felt soaked from head to toe.

That's what she got for racing away from the camp in Puerto Grande the way she had. If she'd stopped to think longer, she might have at least brought along some warmer clothes to wear beneath the rain poncho.

Instead, she'd given All-Med's team leader, Dr. Miguel Chavez, a hasty excuse that a friend in Caracas had an emergency, and off she'd gone with Brody in this miserable excuse of a vehicle. She knew they wouldn't expect her back anytime soon. In *good* weather, Caracas was a day away.

"The convent where the kids were left is up this road," he said, still drumming. If he was as uncomfortable with the conditions as she, he hid it well. "There's no other access to St. Agnes's. Unless a person was airlifted in. And *that* ain't gonna happen in this weather." His head bounced a few times, as if he were mentally agreeing with whatever other insane thoughts were bouncing around inside.

She angled her legs in the hard, ripped seat, turning her back against the driving rain. "If we walked, we could make it back to the camp at Puerto Grande before dark." Though dark was a subjective term, considering the oppressive clouds that hung over their heads.

Since she'd turned twenty, she'd visited Venezuela with All-Med five times, but this was the worst weather she'd ever encountered.

"Only way we're going is forward, sweetie." He sighed loud enough to be heard above the rain that was pounding on the roof of the vehicle. His jeans and rain poncho were caked with mud from his repeated attempts to dislodge the Jeep.

"But the convent is still *miles* away." They were much closer to the camp where she'd been stationed. "We could get some help from the team tomorrow. Work the Jeep free of the mud. They wouldn't have to know that we were trying to get up to St. Agnes instead of to Caracas."

"Can't afford to waste that much time."

She huffed out a breath and stared at the man. He truly gave new meaning to the word stubborn.

She angled her back even farther against the blowing wind. Her knees brushed against the gearshift, and when she tried to avoid that, they brushed against his thigh.

If that fact was even noticeable to him, he gave no indication whatsoever. So she left her knee right where it was, since the contact provided a nice little bit of warmth to her otherwise shivering body.

Shivers caused by cold *and* an uncomfortable suspicion she'd had since he unexpectedly appeared in Puerto Grande.

"What's the rush?" she asked. "You told me we were merely picking up the Stanley kids from the convent for their parents."

"We are."

Her lips tightened. "Brody—"

"I told you to call me Hewitt, remember?"

There was nothing particularly wrong with the name, but he definitely didn't seem a "Hewitt" type to her. Brody was energy itself all contained within long legs, long hands and a hard body. If she had to be stuck in the mud at the base of a mountain in a foreign country, she supposed Brody was about the best companion she could have. She wouldn't go so far as to call the man *safe,* but she did believe he was capably creative when the situation called for it.

"Fine, *Hewitt,*" she returned, "so what's the rush? The children have been at the convent for nearly two months. What's one more night?" He'd already filled her in on the details of how Hewitt Stanley—the real Hewitt Stanley—and his wife, Sophia, had tucked their two children in the small, exceedingly reclusive convent while they trekked deep into the most unreachable portions of Venezuela to further their latest pharmaceutical quest.

Brody had, supposedly, enlisted Angeline's help because he claimed he couldn't manage retrieving both kids on his own.

"The Santina Group kidnapped Hewitt and Sophia two days ago."

"Excuse me?"

Despite the rough beard, his profile as he peered through the deluged windshield could have been chiseled from the mountains around them. "Do you ever wonder about the messages you're asked to dispatch?"

"No."

"Never." He gave her another one of those mind reader looks.

Sometimes, honesty was a darned nuisance.

"Yes. Of course I am curious sometimes," she admitted. "But I don't make any attempt to satisfy that curiosity. That's not my role.

I'm just the messenger. And what does that have to do with the Stanleys?"

He raised one eyebrow. "When I gave you that intel back in November, you didn't wonder about it?" He didn't quite sound disbelieving, but the implication was there.

"There are lots of things I wonder about, but I don't have the kind of clearance to know more. Maybe I prefer it that way." The tidbits of information that she dispatched were not enough to give her real knowledge of the issues that Hollins-Winword handled. It was a tried-and-true safety measure, not only for her personal safety, but for those around her, the agency's work and the agency itself.

She knew that. Understood that. Welcomed it, even.

She believed in her involvement with Hollins-Winword. But that didn't mean she was anxious to risk her neck over four sentences, which was generally the size of the puzzle pieces of information with which she was entrusted. Brody's message for her that night at Leandra and Evan's wedding reception had been even briefer.

Stanley experimenting. Sandoval MIA.

She'd memorized the information—

hardly difficult in this case—and shortly after she'd returned to Atlanta, she'd relayed the brief missive to the impossibly young-looking boy who'd spilled his backpack on the floor next to her table at a local coffee shop.

She'd knelt down beside him and helped as he'd packed up his textbooks, papers and pens, and three minutes later, he was heading out the door with his cappuccino and the message, and she was sitting back down at her table with her paperback book and her latte.

"You didn't look twice at the name Sandoval."

Somehow, cold water had snuck beneath the neck of her poncho and was dripping down the back of her spine. She tugged the hood of her poncho farther over her forehead but it was about as effective as closing the barn door after the horse was already out, considering the fact that she was already soaked. "Does it matter? Sandoval's not that unusual of a name."

His lips twisted. "How old were you when you left Santo Marguerite?"

The kernel inside her suddenly exploded, turning tense curiosity into a sickening fear that she didn't want to acknowledge. "Four." Old enough to remember that the name of the man who'd destroyed the Central American village where she'd been born, along with nearly everyone else who'd lived there, had been Sandoval.

She reached out and closed her hand over his slick, wet forearm. "I'm no good at guessing games, Brody. Just tell me what you want me to know. Is Sandoval involved with the kidnapping?"

His gaze flicked downward, as if surprised by the contact, and she hastily drew back, curling her cold hands together.

"We haven't been able to prove it, but we believe that he is the money behind the Santina Group. On the other hand, we *know* Santina funds at least two different black market organizations running everything from drugs and weapons to human trafficking. According to the pharmaceutical company Hewitt works for, he was on to something huge. Has to do with some little red frog about the size of my fingernail."

He shook his head, as if the entire matter was unfathomable to him. "Anyway, the pharmacy folks will try to replicate synthetically the properties of this frog spit, or whatever the *hell* it is." His voice went terse. "And in the right hands, that's fine. But those properties are *also* the kind of properties that in the wrong hands, could bring a whole new meaning to what profit is in the drug trade."

"They've got the parents and now they're after the kids, too. Sandoval or Santina or whoever," she surmised, feeling even more appalled.

"We're working on that theory. One of Santina's top men—Rico Fuentes—was spotted in Caracas yesterday morning. Sophia Stanley's parents were Venezuelan, and she inherited a small apartment there when they died. The place was tossed yesterday afternoon."

"How can you be sure the kids are even at the convent?"

"Because *I* tossed the apartment yesterday *morning* and found Sophia's notes she'd made about getting there, and packing clothes and stuff for the kids. I didn't leave anything for ol' Rico to find but who knows who Hewitt and Sophia may have told about their kids' whereabouts. I've got my people talking to everyone at the pharmaceutical place, and so far none of them seems to know anything about the convent, but…" He shrugged and looked back at the road.

"Hewitt obviously knew they were on to something that would be just as significant to the bad guys as to the good," he told her. "Otherwise, why squirrel away their kids the way they did? They could have just hired a nanny to mind them while they went exploring in the tepuis." He referred to the unearthly, flattop mountains located in the remote southeast portion of the country. She knew the region was inhabited by some extremely unusual life-forms.

"Instead," he went on, "they used the convent where Sophia's mother once spent time as a girl."

"If this Rico person gets to the children, Santina could use them as leverage to make sure Hewitt cooperates."

"Bingo."

"What about Hewitt and Sophia, though? How will they even know their kids are still safe? Couldn't these Santina group people lie?"

"Hell yeah, they could lie. They *will* lie. But there's another team working on their rescue. Right now, we need to make certain that whatever threats made concerning those kids *are* a lie."

She blew out a long breath. "Why not go to the authorities? Surely they'd be of more help."

"Which local authorities do you think we can implicitly trust?"

She frowned. Miguel had often complained about the thriving black market and its rumored connection to the local police. "Brody, this kind of thing is way beyond me. I'm not a field agent. You know that better than anyone." Her involvement with Hollins-Winword had only ever involved the transmittal of information!

A deep crevice formed down his cheek as the corner of his lips lifted. "You are now, sweet cheeks."

"I do have a name," she reminded.

"Yeah. And until we get the kids outta this country, it's Sophia Stanley."

"I beg your pardon?"

"Beg all you want. There's a packet in the glove box."

She fumbled with the rusting button and managed to open the box. It was stuffed with maps and an assortment of hand tools. The packet, she assumed, was the dingy envelope wedged between a long screwdriver and a bundle of nylon rope. She pulled it out and lifted the flap. Inside was a narrow gold ring with a distinctive pattern engraved on it and several snapshots.

He took the envelope and turned the contents out into his hand. "Here." He handed her the ring. "Put this on."

She gingerly took the ring from him and started to slide it on her right hand.

He shook his head. "Left hand. It's a wedding ring, baby cakes."

Feeling slightly sick to her stomach, she pushed the gold band over her cold wedding-ring finger. It was a little loose. She curled her fingers into her palm, holding it in place.

She'd never put a ring on that particular finger before, and it felt distinctly odd.

"This," he held up a picture, "is Sophia."

A laughing woman with long dark hair smiled at the camera. She looked older than Angeline, but overall, their coloring was nearly identical, from their olive-toned skin to their dark brown eyes.

"Not a perfect match," Brody said. "You're prettier. But you'll have to do."

She frowned, not sure if that was a compliment or not, but he took no notice.

"These are the kids. Eva's nine. Davey's four." He handed her a few more pictures, barely giving her time to examine one before handing her the next. "And this is papa bear."

If the situation hadn't been as serious as she knew it was, she would have laughed right out loud. The real Hewitt Stanley definitely matched the mental image his name conjured.

Medium height. Gangly and spectacled. Even from the snapshot, slightly blurred though it was, the man's *un*-Brody-ness shined through. Other than the fact that they were both male, there was nothing remotely similar between the two men. "*This* is who you're pretending to be."

"You'd be surprised at the identities I've assumed," he said, taking back the photographs when she handed them to him. He tucked them back in the envelope, which then disappeared beneath his rain poncho.

"Why do we even need to pretend to be the Stanleys, anyway? The nuns at the convent will surely know we're *not* the people who left their children in their safekeeping."

"Generally, the Mother Superior deals with

outsiders. She's definitely the only one who would have met with Hewitt and Sophia when they took in the children. And she's currently stuck in Puerto Grande thanks to the weather that *we* are not going to let stop us."

"Maybe we can fool a few nuns," she hesitated for a moment, rather expecting a bolt of lightning to strike at the very idea of it, "but the kids will know we're not their parents. They will certainly have something to say about going off with two complete strangers."

"The Stanleys had a code word for their kids. Falling waters. When we get that to them, they'll know we're there on behalf of their parents."

The situation could not possibly become anymore surreal. "How do you know *that?*"

"Because I do. Believe me, if I thought we could just walk into that convent up there and tell the nuns we were taking the kids away for their own safety, I would. But there's a reason Hewitt and Sophia chose the place. It's hellacious to reach, even on a good day. It's cloistered. It's small; barely even a dot on the satellite imaging."

Again she felt that panicky feeling starting to crawl up her throat. "W-what if we fail?"

The last time she'd failed had been in Atlanta, and it hadn't had anything to do with Hollins-Winword. But it had certainly involved a child.

He gave her a sidelong look. "We won't."

"Why didn't you tell me all this when you showed up at the aid camp?" If he had, she would have found some reason to convince him to find someone else.

"Too many ears." He reached beneath his seat and pulled out a handgun. So great was her surprise, she barely recognized it as a weapon.

In a rapid movement he checked the clip and tucked the gun out of sight where he'd put the envelope of photographs beneath his rain poncho.

She'd grown up on a ranch, so she wasn't unfamiliar with firearms. But the presence of rifles and shotguns hanging in the gun case in her father's den was a far cry from the thing that Brody had just hidden away. "We won't need that though, right?"

"Let's hope not." He gave her a look, as if he knew perfectly well how she felt about getting into a situation where they might. "I don't want to draw down on a nun anymore than the next guy. If we can convince them we're Hewitt and Sophia Stanley, we won't have to. But believe me, sweet cheeks, they're better off if I resort to threats than if Santina's guy does. They don't draw the line over hurting innocent people. And if we're not as far ahead of the guy as I hope, you're going to be pretty happy that I've got—" he patted his side "—good old Delilah with us, sweet cheeks."

He named his gun Delilah?

She shook her head, discomfited by more than just the gun.

Sandoval certainly hadn't drawn the line over hurting people, she knew. Not when she'd been four and the man had destroyed her family's village in a power struggle for control of the verdant land. When he'd been in danger of losing the battle, he'd destroyed the land, too, rather than let someone beat him.

"It's not sweet cheeks," she said, and blamed her shaking voice on the cold water still sneaking beneath her poncho. "It's Sophia."

Brody slowly smiled. "That's my girl."

She shivered again and knew, that time, that it wasn't caused entirely by cold or nerves.

It was caused by *him*.

Chapter Two

They abandoned the Jeep where it was mired in the mud and proceeded on foot.

It seemed to take hours before they managed to climb their way up the steep, slick mountainside.

The wind swirled around them, carrying the rain in sheets that were nearly horizontal. Angeline felt grateful for Brody's big body standing so closely to hers, blocking a fair measure of the storm.

She lost all sense of time as they trudged along. Every step she took was an exercise in pain—her thighs, her calves, her shins. No part of her seemed excused until finally—when her brain had simply shut down except for the mental order to keep moving, keep moving, keep moving—Brody stopped.

He lifted his hand, and beat it hard on the wide black plank that barred their path.

A door, her numb mind realized. "They won't hear," she said, but couldn't even hear the words herself over the screaming wind.

His fingers were an iron ring around her wrist as the door creaked open—giving lie to her words—and he pulled her inside. Then he put his shoulder against the door and muscled it closed again, yanking down the old-fashioned wooden beam that served as a lock.

The sudden cessation of battering wind was nearly dizzying.

It was also oddly quiet, she realized. So much so that she could hear the water dripping off her onto the stone floor.

"*Señora.*" A diminutive woman dressed in a full nun's habit held out a white towel.

"Thank you." Angeline took the towel and pressed it to her face. The weave was rough and thin but it was dry and felt positively wonderful. She lowered it to smile at the nun. *"Gracias."*

The woman was speaking rapidly to Brody in Spanish. And though Angeline hadn't spoken the language of her birth in years, she followed along easily enough. The nun was telling Brody that the Mother Superior was not there to welcome the strangers.

"We're not strangers," Brody told her. His accent was nearly flawless, Angeline realized with some vague surprise. "We've come to collect our children."

If Angeline had held any vague notions of other children being at the convent, they were dissolved when the nun nodded. *"Sí. Sí."* The nun turned and began moving away from the door, heading down the middle of the three corridors that led off the vestibule.

Brody gave Angeline a sharp look when she didn't immediately follow along.

She knew she could collapse later, *after* they knew the children were safe. But just then she wanted nothing more than to just sink down on the dark stone floor and rest her head back against the rough, white-washed wall.

As if he could read her thoughts, Brody

wrapped his hand around her wrist again and drew her along the corridor with him in the nun's wake.

Like the vestibule, the hallway had whitewashed walls. Though the wash looked pristine, it didn't mask the rough texture of the wall beneath it. There were no windows, but a multitude of iron sconces situated high up the wall held fat white candles that kept the way well lit. The few electrical sconces spread out less liberally were dark.

Angeline figured they'd walked a good fifty feet before the corridor turned sharply left and opened after another twenty or so feet into a wide, square room occupied by a half-dozen long wooden tables and benches.

The dining hall, the nun informed them briskly. Her feet didn't hesitate, however, as she kept right on walking.

"You catching all that?" Brody asked Angeline in English.

She nodded. She'd come to English only when Daniel and Maggie Clay had adopted her after her family's village was destroyed. And though Angeline had deliberately turned her back on the language of her natural parents, she'd never forgotten it, though she'd once made a valiant effort to do so.

She'd already been different enough from the other people in that small Wyoming town where she'd gone to live with Daniel and Maggie. Even before she'd been old enough to understand her actions, she'd deliberately rid the accent from her diction, and copied the vague drawl that the adults around her had possessed. She'd wanted so badly to belong. Not because any one of her adopted family made her feel different, but because inside, Angeline had known she *was* different.

She'd lived when the rest of her natural family had perished. She'd been rescued from a poor Central American orphanage and been taken to the U.S., where she'd been raised by loving people.

But she'd never forgotten the sight of fire racing through the fields her cousins had tended, licking up the walls and across the roofs of their simple houses. And whatever hadn't been burned had been hacked down with axes, torn apart with knives, shot down with guns.

Nothing had escaped. Not the people. Not the livestock. Not the land.

Only *her.*

It was twenty-five years ago, and she still didn't understand why she'd been spared.

"Sophia." Brody's voice was sharp, cutting through the dark memories. Angeline focused on his deep blue eyes and just that abruptly she was back in the present.

Where two children needed them.

"I'm sorry." How easily she fell back into thinking in Spanish, speaking in Spanish. "The children," she looked at the nun. "Please, where are they?"

The nun looked distressed. "They are well and safe, *señora*. But until the Mother Superior returns and authorizes your access to them, I must continue to keep them secure."

"From me?" Angeline didn't have to work hard at conjuring tears in her eyes. She was cold, exhausted and entirely undone by the plot that Brody had drawn her into. "I am their mother." The lie came more easily than she'd thought it would.

The nun's ageless face looked pitying, yet resolute. "You were the ones who made the arrangement with Mother. But now, you are weary," she said. "You and your husband need food and rest. We will naturally provide you with both until Mother returns. The storm will pass and soon she will be here to show you to your children."

"But—"

Brody's hand closed around hers. "*Gracias,* Sister. My wife and I thank you for your hospitality, of course. If we could find dry clothes—"

"*Sí. Sí.*" The nun looked relieved. "Please wait here. I will send Sister Frances to assist you in a moment if that will be satisfactory?"

Brody's fingers squeezed Angeline's in warning "*Sí.*"

She nodded and turned on her heel, gliding back along the corridor. Her long robes swished over the stone floor.

The moment she was out of sight, Brody let go of Angeline's wrist and she sank down onto one of the long wooden benches situated alongside the tables. She rubbed her wrist, flushing a little when she realized he was watching the action. She stopped, telling herself inwardly that her skin wasn't *really* tingling.

What was one more lie there inside that sacred convent, considering the whoppers they were already telling?

Brody sat down beside her and she wanted to put some distance between them given the way he was crowding into her personal space, but another nun—presumably Sister Frances—silently entered the dining area. She gestured for Brody and Angeline to follow, and Brody tucked his hand beneath Angeline's arm as he helped her solicitously to her feet.

They followed the silent nun down another corridor and up several narrow flights of stairs, all lit with those same iron wall sconces. Finally she stopped and opened a heavy wooden door, extending her hand in a welcoming gesture. Clearly they were meant to go inside.

Angeline passed the nun, thanking her quietly as she entered the room. Brody ducked his head to keep from knocking it against the low sill and followed her inside. The dim room contained a single woefully narrow bed, a single straight-backed wooden chair and a dresser with an old-fashioned ceramic pitcher and basin atop it.

The nun reached up to the sconce on the wall outside the door and pulled down the lit candle, handing it to Brody. She waved her hand toward the two sconces inside the bedroom, and Brody reached up, setting the flame to the candles they contained.

Warm light slowly filled the tiny room as the flames caught. Brody handed the feeder candle back to the nun, who nodded and backed two steps out of the room, pulling the wooden door shut as she went.

Which left Angeline alone with Brody.

The room had no windows, and though Angeline was definitely no fan of small, enclosed spaces, the room simply felt cozy. Cozy and surprisingly safe, considering the surreal situation.

"Well," he said in a low tone, "that was easier than I expected."

She gaped. "Easy? They won't even let us *see* the children."

"Shh." He lifted one of the candles from its sconce and began prowling around the room's small confines.

She lowered her voice. "What are you looking for?"

He ignored her. He nudged the bed away from the wall. Looked behind it. Under it. Pushed it back. He did the same with the dresser. He turned the washbasin and the pitcher upside down, before replacing them atop the dresser. He even pulled the unlit bare lightbulb out of the metal fixture hanging from the low ceiling. Then, evidently with nothing else to examine, he returned the fat candle to the sconce.

"Don't think we're being bugged."

Her lips parted. "Seriously?"

"I'm a big believer in paranoia." He looked up at the steady candle flames. "Walls in this place must be about a foot deep," he said. "Can hardly hear the storm out there."

And she was closed within them with *him* in a room roughly the size of the balcony of her Atlanta apartment. "Sorry if I'm not quick on the uptake here. Is that supposed to be good or bad?"

He shrugged, and began pulling off his rain poncho, doing a decent job of not flinging mud onto the white blanket covering the bed. "It ain't bad," he said when his head reappeared. "At least we probably don't have to worry about that hurricane blowing this place to bits." He dropped the poncho in the corner behind the door. The Rolling Stones T-shirt he wore beneath it was as lamentably wet as her own, and he lifted the hem, pulling the gun and its holster off his waistband.

He tucked them both beneath the mattress.

"Probably," she repeated faintly. "Bro—Hewitt, what about the children?"

"We'll get to them," he said.

She wished she felt even a portion of the confidence he seemed to feel. "What happened to that all-fire rush you were feeling earlier?"

"Believe me, it's still burning. But first things first." His long arm came up, his hand brushing her poncho and she nearly jumped out of her skin. "Relax. I was just gonna help you take off your poncho."

She felt her cheeks heat and was grateful for the soft candlelight that would hide her flush. "I knew that."

He snorted softly.

Fortunately, she was saved from further embarrassment when there was a soft knock on the door.

It only took Brody two steps to reach it, and when it swung open, yet another nun stood on the threshold carrying a wooden tray. She smiled faintly and tilted her head, her black veil swishing softly. But like the sister who'd shown them to the room, she remained silent as she set the tray on the dresser top and began unloading it.

A simple woven basket of bread. A hunk of cheese. A cluster of green grapes. Two thick white plates, a knife, two sparkling clear glasses and a fat round pitcher. All of it she left on the dresser top. She didn't look at Brody and Angeline as she bowed her head over the repast.

She was obviously giving a blessing. Then she lifted her head, smiled peacefully again and returned to the door. She knelt down, picked up a bundle she'd left outside, and brought it in, setting it on the bed. Then she let herself out of the room. Like Sister Frances, she pulled the door shut as she went.

"Grub and fresh duds," Brody said, looking happy as a pig in clover. He lifted the off-white bundle from the bed and the items separated as he gave it a little shake. "Pants and top for you. Pants and top for me." He deftly sorted, and tossed the smaller set toward the two thin pillows that sat at the head of the modest bed.

She didn't reach for them, though.

He angled her a look. "Don't worry, beautiful. I'll turn my back while you change." His lips twitched. "There's not even a mirror in here for me to take a surreptitious peek.

Now if you feel so compelled, *you're* welcome to look all you want. After all," his amused voice was dry, "we are married."

Her cheeks heated even more. "Stop. Please. My sides are splitting because you are sooo funny."

His lips twitched again and he pulled his T-shirt over his head.

Angeline swallowed, not looking away quickly enough to miss the ripped abdomen and wealth of satin-smooth golden skin stretched tightly across a chest that hadn't looked nearly so wide in the shirt he'd worn. When his hands dropped to the waist of his jeans, she snatched up the clean, dry clothing and turned her back on him.

Then just when she wished the ground would swallow her whole, she heard his soft, rumbling chuckle.

She told herself to get a grip. She was a paramedic for pity's sake. She'd seen nude men, women and children in all manner of situations.

There's a difference between nude and naked, a tiny voice inside her head taunted, and Brody's bare chest was *all* about being naked.

She silenced the voice and snatched her

shirt off over her head, dropping it in a sopping heap on the floor. Leaving on her wet bra would only make the dry top damp, so she snapped it off, too, imaging herself anywhere but in that confining room with Brody Paine. She pulled the dry top over her head.

She tried imagining that she was a quick-change artist as she yanked the tunic firmly over her hips—grateful that it reached her thighs—then ditched her own wet jeans and panties for the dry pants.

She immediately felt warmer.

She knelt down and bundled her filthy clothes together, tucking away the scraps of lace and satin lingerie inside.

"Trying to hide the evidence that you like racy undies?"

Her head whipped around and the towel tumbled off her head.

Brody was facing her, hip propped against the dresser, arms crossed over the front of the tunic that strained slightly in the shoulders. He had an unholy look in his eyes that ought to have had the storm centering all of her fury on them considering their surroundings.

"You promised not to look."

His mobile lips stretched, revealing the

edge of his very straight, very white teeth. "Babe, you sound prim enough to be one of the sisters cloistered here."

Her cheeks couldn't possibly get any hotter. "Which doesn't change the fact that you promised."

He lifted one shoulder. "Promises are made to be broken."

"You don't really believe that."

"How do you know?"

It couldn't possibly be anymore obvious. "It doesn't matter how many lines you give me, because the truth is, you couldn't do the work you do if you didn't believe in keeping your word," she said simply.

Chapter Three

Brody looked at Angeline's face. She looked so… earnest, he thought. Earnest and sexy as hell in a way that had *nothing* to do with those hanks of black lace he'd gotten a glimpse of.

She'd always been a deadly combination, even in the small doses of time they'd ever spent together.

Was it any wonder that he'd been just as interested in consuming a larger dose as he'd been in avoiding just that?

Complications on the job were one thing.

Complications off the job were nonexistent because that's the way he kept it.

Always.

But there she was, watching him with those huge, wide-set brown eyes that had gotten to him even on their first, ridiculously brief encounter five years earlier.

He deliberately lifted one eyebrow. "It's a job, sweet cheeks. A pretty well-paying one."

"Assembling widgets is a job," she countered. "Protecting the innocent? Righting wrongs? That's not just a job and somehow I doubt you do it only for the money."

"You're not just prim, you're a romantic, too," he drawled.

She frowned a little, possibly realizing the topic had gone somewhat awry. "So what's the next step?"

He held up a cluster of grapes. "We eat."

Right on cue, her stomach growled loud enough for him to hear. "Shouldn't we try to find the children?"

"You wanna pull off our own kidnapping?" He wasn't teasing.

"That's essentially what your plan *was*."

"I'd consider it more a case of protective custody."

She pushed her fingers through her hair, holding it back from her face. She didn't have on a lick of makeup, and she was still more beautiful than ninety-nine percent of the world's female population.

"Fine. Call it whatever," she dismissed. "Shouldn't we be doing something to that end?"

"I told you. First things first. How far do you think we'll get if we set out right this second? You're so exhausted I can see the circles under your eyes even in *this* light and I'm not sure who's stomach is growling louder. Yours or mine." He popped a few grapes into his mouth and held up the cluster again. "Come on, darlin'. Eat up."

"I think we should at least try to see the children. What if that password thing doesn't work?" But she plucked a few grapes off the cluster and slid one between her full bow-shaped lips. She chewed and swallowed, and avoiding his eyes, quickly reached for more.

"It will." He tore off a chunk of the bread and handed it to her, and cut the wedge of cheese in half. "Here."

She sat on the foot of the bed and looked as if she was trying not to wolf down the food. He tipped the pitcher over one of the glasses, filling it with pale golden liquid. He took a sniff. "Wine." He took a drink. "Pretty decent wine at that." He poured the second glass and held it out to her.

She took it from him, evidently too thirsty to spend a lot of effort avoiding brushing his fingers the way she usually did. "Wine always goes straight to my head."

"Goody goody." He tossed one of the cloth napkins that had been tucked beneath the bread basket onto her lap. "Drink faster."

She let out an impatient laugh. "Do you *ever* stop with the come-ons?"

"Do you *ever* take me up on one?"

She made a face at him. "Why would I want to be just another notch?"

"Who says that's what you'd be?"

She took another sip of wine. "I'm sure that's the only thing women are to you."

"I'm wounded, babe. You're different than all the others."

She let out a half laugh. "You are so full of it."

"And you are way too serious." He bit into a hunk of bread. He was thirty-eight years old—damn near a decade her senior—but he might as well have been sixteen given the way he kept getting preoccupied with that narrow bed where she was gingerly perched.

"I'm a serious person," she said around a not-entirely delicate mouthful of bread. "In a serious business."

"The paramedic business or the spy business?"

"I'm not a spy."

He couldn't help smiling again. "Sugar, you're a courier for one of the biggies in the business." He tipped more wine into his glass. "And your family just keeps getting pulled in, one way or the other."

"You ought to know. You're the one who approached me in the first place to be a courier."

He couldn't dispute that. "Still. Don't you think it's a little…unusual?"

She didn't even blink. "You mean how many of us are involved with Hollins-Winword?"

At least she wasn't as in the dark as her cousin Sarah had been. Sarah'd had no clue that she wasn't the only one in her family hooked up with Hollins-Winword; probably wouldn't know even now if her brand-spank-ing-new husband, Max Scalise, hadn't tramped one of his own investigations right through Brody's assignment to protect a little girl named Megan. They'd been staying in a safe house in Weaver, set up by Sarah, who mostly made her living as a school teacher when she wasn't making an occasional "arrangement" for Hollins-Winword. But she'd only learned that her uncles were involved. She hadn't learned about Angeline.

Or the others in that extensive family tree.

And now, he'd heard that Sarah and Max were in the process of adopting Megan.

The child's parents had been brutally murdered, but she'd at least have some chance at regaining a decent life with decent people raising her.

She'd have a family.

The thought was darker than it should have been and he reached for the wine pitcher again, only to find it empty. Thirty-eight years old, horny, thirsty and feeling envious of some innocent, eight-year-old kid.

What the hell was wrong with him? He'd been several years older than Megan had been when his real family had been blown to bits. As for the "family" he'd had after that, he'd hardly term a hard-assed workaholic like Cole as real.

Sitting across from him on the foot of the bed, Angeline had spread out the napkin over her lap, and as he watched, she delicately brushed her fingertips over the cloth.

She had the kind of hourglass figure that men fantasized over, a Madonna's face and fingers that looked like they should have nothing more strenuous to do than hold up beautifully jeweled rings. Yet twice now, he'd found her toiling away in the ass-backwards village of Puerto Grande.

That first time, five years ago, his usual courier had missed the meet and Brody had been encouraged to develop a new asset. And oh, by the way, isn't it convenient that there's a pretty American in Puerto Grande whose family is already involved with Hollins-Winword.

The situation had always struck Brody as too convenient for words. But he'd gone ahead and done his job. He'd talked her into the gig, passed off the intel that she was to relay later when she was back in the States and voilà, her career as a courier was born.

The second time he'd found her working like a dog in Puerto Grande had been, of course, just that morning. He'd called in to his handler at Hollins-Winword to find out who he could pull in fast to assist him on getting the kids, only to learn that, lo and behold, once again the lovely Señorita Clay was right there in Puerto Grande. She would be the closest, quickest—albeit unlikely—assistant. And one he'd had to think hard and fast whether he wanted joining him or not. Desperate measures, though, had him going for it.

Not that it had been easy to convince her to join him. As she'd said, she wasn't a field agent. Not even close. Her experience in such matters was nil. *And* she had her commitment to All-Med to honor. The small medical team was administering vaccinations and treating various ailments of the villagers around Puerto Grande.

He'd had to promise that another volunteer would arrive shortly to replace her before she'd made one single move toward his Jeep.

She was definitely a woman of contrasts.

When she wasn't pulling some humanitarian aid stint, she worked the streets of Atlanta as a paramedic, yet usually talked longingly of the place she'd grown up in: Wyoming.

And there wasn't a single ring—jeweled or otherwise—on those long, elegant fingers, except the wedding band that had been his mother's.

Usually, he kept it tucked in his wallet. As a reminder never to get too complacent with life. Too comfortable. Too settled.

Considering how settled he'd been becoming lately, maybe it was a timely reminder.

"Do you remember much of Santo Marguerite?"

Her lashes lifted as she gave him a startled look. Just as quickly, those lush lashes lowered again. She lifted one shoulder and the crisp fabric of the tunic slipped a few inches, giving him a better view of the hollow at the base of that long, lovely throat.

"I remember it a little." She pleated the edge of the napkin on her lap then leaned forward to retrieve the wineglass that she'd set on the floor. "What do you even know about the place? It no longer exists."

She had a point. What he knew he'd learned from *her* file at Hollins-Winword. The dwellings of the village that had been destroyed were never rebuilt, though Sandoval had been in control of the land for the last few

decades, guarding it with the violent zeal-
ousness he was known for.

She evidently took his silence as his
answer. "Where did *you* grow up?" she asked.

"Here and there." He straightened from his
perch and stretched. Talking about her past
was one thing. His was off-limits. Even he
tried not to think about it. "You figure that
bed's strong enough to hold us both?"

Her eyes widened a fraction before she
looked away again. "I...I'm used to roughing
it in camps and such. I can sleep on the floor."

"Hardly sounds like a wifely thing to do."

She scrunched up the napkin and slid off
the bed. "I'm not a wife."

"Shh." There was something wrong with
the way he took such pleasure in seeing the
dusky color climb into that satin-smooth
complexion of hers.

Her lips firmed. "You've already estab-
lished that these walls don't have ears."

"So I did. Kind of a pity, really. I was
looking forward to seeing how well we
played mister and missus for the night."

Giving him a frozen look, she polished off
the rest of her wine. Then she just stood there,
staring at the blank wall ahead of her.

In the candlelight, her hair looked dark as ink against the pale cloth of her tunic, though he knew in the sunlight, those long gleaming locks were not really black at all, but a deep, lustrous brown.

"Whatcha thinking?"

She didn't look back at him. She folded her arms over her chest. Her fingertips curled around her upper arms and he saw the wink of candlelight catching in the gold wedding band. "I wonder why they don't have windows here."

"Considering the way the weather was blowing out there, that's probably a blessing about now." He watched her back for a moment. The tunic reached well below her hips, and though he'd always had the impression of her being very tall, he knew that it was merely the way she carried herself. Not that she was short, but he had her by a good seven or eight inches. And there, in that tunic and pants, her feet bare, she seemed much less Wonder Woman than usual.

Vulnerable. That was the word.

She looked vulnerable.

It wasn't necessarily a comfortable realization.

"You claustrophobic?"

She stiffened and shot him a suspicious look. "Why?"

"Just curious." Though the walls in the room were probably going to feel mighty closed in the longer they were confined together with that single, narrow bed.

Her hands rubbed up and down her arms. "The electricity here would be from a generator, wouldn't it?"

"I'd think so, though that doesn't explain why it's not running. Maybe they've got concerns with the gas it would take. Why? You cold?"

"Some. You, um, you suppose there's plumbing here?"

He hid a smile. The convent was cloistered, and located in a highly remote location. But it wasn't entirely out of the middle ages. "This is built like a dorm," he said. "I saw the bathroom a floor down."

She dropped her arms, casting him a relieved look. "You did?"

"Probably better facilities here than you had in that hut at Puerto Grande." He reached for the door. "After you, my darling wife."

When they got to the bathroom door, Brody stopped. "Place is built for women," he reminded her. "You'd better go first. Make sure I don't send some poor nun into heart failure."

"I won't be long." She ducked inside.

In his experience, women were forever finding reasons to spend extra time in the bathroom. Lord only knew what they did in there.

But she did open the door again, almost immediately. "All clear." She slipped past him back into the corridor and he went inside.

The halls were still silent when they made their way back up the narrow staircase and to the room. They passed a half-dozen other doors as they went. All closed.

"Where do you suppose the children are?"

He wished that he had a good answer. "We'll find out soon enough."

"I don't understand why you're still feeling so awfully patient, considering your hurry to get up here."

"Honey, I'm not patient. But I am practical."

She stopped. "What's so practical about getting all the way here, with no means of getting back *out* of here?"

"Oh, ye of little faith." He caught a

glimpse of swishing black fabric from the corner of his eye.

"Bro—"

He pulled Angeline to him and planted his mouth over hers, cutting off his name.

She gave out a shocked squeak and went ramrod stiff. Her hands found their way to his chest, pushing, and he closed his hands around hers, squeezing them in warning.

She went suddenly soft, and instead of fighting him, she kissed him back.

It took more than a little effort for him to remember the kiss was only for the benefit of the nun, and damned if he didn't feel a few bubbles off center when he managed to drag his mouth from those delectably soft lips and give the sister—Sister Frances, in fact—an embarrassed, Hewitt-type apology.

She tilted her head slightly. "The sacrament of marriage is a blessing, *señor.* There is no need for apology." Her smile took in them both. "You will be comfortable for the night? Is there anything else we can provide for you?"

He kept his hands around Angeline's. "A visit with our children would be nice."

"I'm sorry. The Reverend Mother must return first."

Angeline tugged her hands out of his. "We understand, Sister. But won't you tell them that we're here for them? That we'll be going home just as soon as we can?"

"Of course, *señora*. They will be delighted." She gave them a kind look. "Rest well. The storm will hopefully have passed by morning and Mother will be able to return." She headed down the hall toward the staircase.

Brody tugged Angeline back into their room and closed the door.

The second he did, she turned on him. "You didn't need to do that."

"Do what?"

Her lips parted. She practically sputtered before any actual words came out. "Kiss me."

He slid his hand over her shoulder and lowered his head. "Whatever you say, honey."

She shoved at him, and he stepped back, chuckling. "Relax, Sophia. We have the nun's blessing, remember?"

"Very funny." She put as much distance between them as the small room afforded. "I'm not going to have to remind you that no means *no,* am I?"

He started to laugh, but realized that she

was serious. "Lighten up. If I ever get serious about getting you in the sack, you'll know."

"You're impossible."

"Usually," he agreed. He yanked back the cover on the bed, and saw the way she tensed. "And you're acting like some vestal virgin. Relax. You might be the stuff of countless dreams, but I do have *some* control."

Her cheeks weren't just dusky rose now. They were positively red. And her snapping gaze wouldn't meet his as she leaned past him and snatched one of the thin pillows off the mattress. "If you were a gentleman, *you'd* take the floor."

"Babe, I'll be the first one to tell you that I am *not* a gentleman."

"Fine." She tossed the pillow on the floor, and gathered up the top cover from the bed. She flipped it out on the slate by the pillow, and sat down on one edge, drawing the other side over her as she lay down, back toward him.

"You're really going to sleep on the floor."

She twitched the cover up over her shoulder. "Looks that way, doesn't it?"

He didn't know whether to laugh or applaud. "If I needed a shower despite the one that Mother Nature gave us that badly, you could have just told me."

She didn't respond.

He looked at the bed. A thin beige blanket covered the mattress. The remaining pillow looked even thinner and more Spartan now that its mate was tucked between Angeline's dark head and the cold hard floor.

Brody muttered a mild oath—they *were* in a convent, after all, and even he didn't believe in taunting fate quite that much—and grabbed the pillow and blanket from the bed and tossed them down on the ground.

She twisted her head around. "What are you doing now?"

"Evidently being shamed into sleeping on this godforsa— blessed floor." He flipped out the blanket and lowered himself onto it. Sad to say, but nearly every muscle inside him protested the motion. He was in pretty decent shape, but climbing the mountain hadn't exactly been a picnic.

"You don't *have* any shame," she countered.

He made a point of turning his back on her as he lay down, scrunching the pillow beneath his head. The area of floor was significantly narrow, but not so narrow that he couldn't have kept his back from touching hers if he'd so chosen.

He didn't choose.

So much for trying to convince the higher powers that he was entirely decent.

She shifted ever so subtly away from him, until he couldn't feel the warmth of her lithe form against him. He rolled onto his back, closing the gap again.

She huffed a little, then sat up and pushed at him to move over. When he didn't, she scrambled to her feet and stepped over him, reaching back for her bedding.

"Where are you going?" He rolled back onto his side and propped his head on his hand, watching her interestedly.

"Away from *you*," she assured. She flung the cover around her shoulders like an over-sized shawl and climbed onto the bed. "When lightning strikes you down, I don't want to be anywhere near."

Brody smiled faintly. "That's good, because I was beginning to think you were afraid of sleeping with little ol' me."

She huffed. "Please. There is *nothing* little about you."

"Babe. I'm flattered."

She gave him a baleful look that made him want to smile even more. "You know they say the larger the ego, the smaller the, um—"

"Id?" he supplied innocently.

She huffed again and threw herself down on the pillow. "Blow out the candles."

"I thought you'd never ask." He got up and did so, turning the small, cozily lit room into one that was dark as pitch.

She was silent. So silent he couldn't even hear her breathe.

"You all right?"

"It's *really* dark."

He wondered how hard it had been for Angeline to admit that. She damn sure wouldn't appreciate him noticing the hint of vulnerability in her smooth, cool voice.

Two steps to his right and he reached the dresser. The small tin of matches was next to the pitcher and bowl and he found that easily, too. A scrape of the match against the wall, a spit of a spark, the flare of sulfur, and the tiny flame seemed to light up the place again. "I can leave one of the candles lit."

"You said you weren't a gentleman."

He set the flame to one of the candles and shook out the match. "I'm not," he assured.

"Then stop acting like one, because now I *have* to give you room on this bed, too." She moved on the mattress, and the iron frame squeaked softly. She groaned and covered her face with her hand.

He laughed softly. "It's just a few squeaky springs. I doubt any of the good sisters are holding glasses against these thick walls hoping for a listen. You act like you've never shared a bed with a guy before."

She didn't move. Not just that she was still, but that she *really* didn't move.

And for a guy who'd generally considered himself quick on the uptake, he realized that this time he'd been mighty damn slow. "Ah. I...see." Though he didn't. Not really. She was twenty-nine years old. How did a woman—a woman who looked like her, yet, with her intelligence, her caring, her...everything—how the hell did she get to be that age and never sleep with a guy?

"Why are you still—why haven't you ever—oh, hell." Disgruntled more at himself than at her, he scraped his hand down his face. "Forget it. It's none of my business."

"No," she agreed. "It's not. Now, are you going to sleep on the bed or not?"

He snatched up the pillow from the floor and tossed it beside her.

She's a virgin. The thought—more like a taunt—kept circling inside his head. Probably what he got for catching a glimpse of that sexy underwear of hers when he'd promised not to look.

He lay down next to her, and the iron bed gave a raucous groan.

"Not one word," she whispered fiercely.

That worked just fine for him.

Chapter Four

Angeline didn't expect to sleep well.

She knew she'd *sleep,* simply because she'd learned long ago to sleep when the opportunity presented itself. And even though Brody's long body was lying next to hers, his weight indenting the mattress just enough that the only way she could keep from rolling toward him was to hang on to the opposite edge of the mattress, she figured she would still manage to catch some z's.

What she didn't expect, however, was to sleep soundly enough, deeply enough, to miss Brody *leaving* the bed.

Or to find that someone had filled the pitcher on the dresser and laid out a freshly folded hand towel on the dresser top.

Okay. So she'd *really* slept soundly.

Not so unusual, she reasoned, as she dashed chilly water over her face and pressed the towel to her cheeks. Making that climb in the storm had been exhausting.

Or maybe you're more comfortable with Brody than you'd like to admit.

She turned and went out of the room, leaving that annoying voice behind.

As before, the corridor was empty, still lit by candles in the sconces. She went down the stairs, visited the long, vaguely industrial-like restroom and then went searching.

But when she reached the ground floor without encountering the impossible-to-miss dining hall, she knew she'd taken a wrong turn somewhere along the way.

Annoyed with herself, she turned on her heel, intending to head back and make another pass at it, but a muffled sound stopped her in her tracks.

Footsteps?

Nervousness charged through her veins and she tried to shake it off. She was in a convent, for pity's sake. What harm could come to them there?

Even if the nuns realized the identity fraud they were perpetrating, what would they be likely to do about it, other than call the authorities, or kick them out into the storm? It wasn't as if they'd put them in chains in a dungeon.

Nevertheless, Angeline still looked around warily, trying to get her bearings. She went over to the nearest window, but it was too far above her head. She couldn't see out even when she tried to jump up and catch the narrow sill with her fingers. So she stood still, pressing a hand to her thumping heart, willing it to quiet as she listened for another sound, another brush of feet, a swish of long black robes.

But all she heard now was silence. She was listening so hard that when melodious bells began chiming, she very nearly jumped out of her skin.

She leaned back against the roughly textured wall and waited for the chiming to end.

"If you're praying, there's a chapel within spitting distance."

Her heart seemed to seize up for the

eternal moment it took to recognize the deep, male voice.

She opened her eyes and looked at Brody. She came from a family of tall, generally oversized men, much like Brody. And she was used to the odd quietness with which most of them moved. But Brody seemed to take that particular skill to an entirely new level. "It's a good thing my heart is healthy," she told him tartly, "because you could give a person a heart attack the way you sneak around!"

"Who needs to sneak?"

"Evidently *you* do," she returned in the same quiet whisper he was using.

Despite the wrinkles in his gender-neutral tunic and pants, he looked revoltingly fresh, particularly compared to the rode-hard-and-put-up-wet way that she felt.

"Did you know you pretty much sleep like the dead?"

She wasn't going to argue the point with him when ordinarily, as a result of her paramedic training, she was quite a light sleeper. "What are you doing sneaking around? Do you know what time it is?"

"It's almost 3:00 a.m. And what are *you*

doing sneaking around? I've been trying to find you for ten minutes."

"I needed the restroom," she whispered. A portion of the truth at least.

He cocked his head. "You got your boots on. Good." He closed his long fingers around her wrist and started walking along the hallway, sticking his head through doorways as he went. "While you were dreaming of handsome princes, I was scoping out this place. Hard to believe, but the fine sisters have an interesting collection of vehicles."

Her stomach clenched. "You'll ask to borrow one?"

Despite the dim lighting, she could tell that his expression didn't change one iota.

She swallowed a groan. "We can't steal one of their cars," she said under her breath.

"Babe." He sounded wounded. "Steal is a harsh word." He stopped short and she nearly bumped into him. "I like *borrow* better."

"That only works when you intend to ask permission to do so," she pointed out the obvious.

"Details. You're always getting hung up on details." He reached up and plucked a candle out of one of the sconces, then pulled open the door beside him and nudged her through. "I wanna move fast, but we've gotta stay quiet. Think you can manage that?"

Her lips parted. "Yes, I can be quiet," she assured, a little more loudly than she ought.

He raised his eyebrows and she pressed her lips together, miming the turning of a key next to them.

His lips quirked. "Good girl."

The spurt of nervousness she'd felt before was nothing compared to the way she felt now as Brody drew her through the doorway. He stopped long enough to hold the door as it closed without a sound.

After tramping down a warren of alarmingly narrow halls, the tile floor gave way to hard-packed dirt.

She swallowed again, feeling like they were heading down into the bowels of the mountain. "Did you sleep at *all?* How long did it take you to discover this rat maze? Do you even know where we're going?"

He paused again, letting her catch up and the candle flame stopped the wild dance of light it cast on the walls. "Yeah, I slept enough. And yeah, I know where we're going. Don't you trust me? We're going to get the kids and get the hell outta Dodge while the going's good."

"But what about your big first-things-first speech?"

"You slept some, didn't you?" His voice was light. "And ate."

She pressed her lips together, determined not to argue. "Your sudden rush just surprised me," she finally managed stiffly.

"Well, along with their various vehicles," he said in such a reasonable tone that she felt like smacking him, "the fine sisters here have a satellite phone system. Hardly the kind of thing one would expect, but hey. Maybe one of the local politicians figures he's buying his way into heaven or something. Anyway, I checked with my handler. The Stanleys have been moved again. And despite the weather, the Mother Superior has found a guide to get her back to her flock. She's supposed to be here shortly after sunup."

"A guide," Angeline echoed. Her irritation dissolved. "What kind of guide?"

"The kind who won't let a washed-out road get in his way."

"You don't think it's that Rico person who searched Sophia and Hewitt's place?"

His gaze didn't waver.

Dismay congealed inside her stomach. "This is a nightmare."

"Nah. Could be worse. Way worse," he assured.

She looked over her shoulder in the direction from which they'd come. What was worse? Going forward or going back? Either way, she really, *really* wanted to get out of this narrow, closed-in tunnel. She looked back at him only to encounter the look he was giving her—sharp eyed *despite* the gloom. *"What?"*

"You tell me. What's bothering you?"

Aside from the entire situation? She moistened her lips. "I, um, I just don't much care for tunnels."

He held the candle above his head, looking up. Then he moved the candle to one side. And the other.

She knew what he was looking at. The ceiling overhead was stucco. The walls on either side of them were stuccoed, as well. And though the floor was dirt, it wasn't as if it were the kind of dirt that had been on the road where the Jeep had gotten stuck. Her boots had encountered no ruts. It seemed perfectly smooth, perfectly compacted.

Not *exactly* a tunnel.

She knew that's what Brody was thinking.

But "We're almost there," was all he said. "Think you can stand it for another couple minutes?"

Pride lifted her chin if nothing else would. This was part of St. Agnes, not a culvert running beneath the city of Atlanta. "Of course."

He didn't smile. Just gave a single nod and turned forward again.

His simple acceptance of her assurance went considerably further than if he'd taken her hand and drawn her along with him like some frightened child. She focused on watching *him*, rather than the confining space, as they continued their brisk pace.

As he'd promised, it was only a few minutes—if that—before she followed Brody around another corner, up several iron stairs and out into the dark, wet air. A vine-twined trellis overhead kept the drizzling rain from hitting them, though Angeline shivered as the air penetrated her clothes.

Thunder was a steady roll, punctuated by the brilliant flicker of lightning.

She got a quick impression of hedges and

rows of plants. The convent's garden? Surely there would have been an easier route to take.

It was then that Brody took her hand in his, lacing his fingers through hers.

She looked up at him, surprise shooting through her.

"Remember, Sophia," he murmured softly, and squeezed her hand. "Falling waters."

She nodded, and right before her very eyes, Brody's expression changed. His shoulders seemed to shrink, and it was as if he no longer towered over her. He even pulled a pair of wire-rimmed glasses from somewhere and stuck them on his face.

Clearly, he wanted to be prepared in case they were discovered.

She wondered suddenly if he had his gun tucked beneath the wrinkled tunic.

Then he drew her from beneath the awning and they dashed across the thick, wet grass toward the building wing on the far side of the garden. They went in through a narrow door, up a flight of stairs and then Brody stopped next to a door. He pushed it open quietly, and pulled her inside.

The room was nearly identical to the one she and Brody had been given, only here, two narrow beds had been pushed against the walls. Small forms were visible beneath the white blankets.

"Let's get her first." Brody nodded toward the bed with the slightly larger hump beneath the covers. He tucked the candle against the basin and pitcher on the dresser and headed to the bed on the right. He touched the covered mound. "Eva—" his voice was soft "—come on, kiddo, rise and shine."

The girl mumbled and shifted, dragging the blanket nearly over her head.

Brody tried again.

This time, the dark head lifted. But at the sight of the strangers, she sucked in a hard breath and opened her mouth.

"Shh." Brody covered her mouth with his hand. "It's okay. Don't scream."

The girl tried scrambling away from Brody, but he held her fast.

"We're here for your parents," Angeline whispered, aching for the child. "Falling waters, right?" She knew from the pictures that Brody had showed her that the girl was pretty with the petite, refined features of her father and the coloring of her mother. But now, in the dark room above the hand Brody still held over her mouth, her eyes were nothing but wide pools of fear.

At the code the Stanleys had instituted, however, the girl's resistance began to ebb.

Angeline knelt beside the bed, closing her hands gently over the fists Eva had made around the edge of the blanket, and willed the girl to trust them.

"Everything is fine," she promised. "Just fine. We're going to take you to your parents just as soon as we can." She prayed that would come to pass. That the team sent to rescue them would be successful.

Eva slowly blinked.

"You need to stay quiet," Brody told her. "Can you do that?"

Again, she blinked. Finally, she gave a faint nod, and Brody gingerly pulled back his hand.

"Who are you?" Eva's whisper shook.

"He's Brody. I'm Angeline. We're... friends of your parents."

"But Sister Frances told us that our parents were already *here*." She knuckled her eyes. "But she wouldn't let us see them. Davey cried."

"*They* aren't actually here," Angeline explained awkwardly. "We, um, we used your parents' names."

Eva drew her eyebrows together. "But—"

"I need you to wake your brother up," Brody interrupted. He'd moved away from the bed and began silently pulling open dresser drawers. "So he's not so frightened." He pulled out several items of clothing and tossed them onto the bed beside the girl. "Do you two have hiking boots or anything? What about a suitcase?"

She nodded warily. "Under the bed."

Brody dropped down and retrieved the boots. He took one look at the unwieldy suitcase and pushed it back beneath the bed. "Thank God for pillowcases," he muttered, and plucked one of the pillows from behind Eva. He yanked the case off and shoved the clothing inside.

"My parents were working in the tepuis. Why didn't they come themselves? And why did you lie to the sisters?" Eva might only be nine, but she certainly knew how to speak her mind.

"They're still working," Angeline assured, lying right through her teeth and hating every moment of it. She squeezed Eva's fists. "Come on now. Let's get Davey awake."

Eva pushed back the blankets and slid off the bed. The hem of her long nightgown settled around her bare feet as she crossed to the other bed and sat down beside her brother. "Davey." She jiggled him. "Wake up." Her attention hardly left Brody, though, as he moved back to the dresser and found some more items to add to the pillowcase.

Davey sat up, looking bleary-eyed. However, at the sight of two strangers—who definitely weren't the nuns he was used to— he practically buried his head against his sister's side.

Even though he was more than half her size, Eva pulled him onto her lap, circling her arms around him protectively. "Mom and Daddy aren't here, after all," she told him. "But they want us to go home."

Angeline could have applauded. The child was showing much more adaptability than Angeline felt.

"In the dark?" Davey asked. He was as blond as his sister was dark, though from the pictures, Angeline knew his eyes were the same deep brown. "How come?"

Angeline sent a beseeching look toward Brody. He ignored it as he pushed his latest handful of clothing into the pillowcase and crouched next to the bed.

She stifled a sigh and tried to find an explanation that wouldn't scare the children anymore than they already were. "You know that we're here for your parents, but Reverend Mother doesn't know that. She only knows that your folks left you in her care, and she's not to release you to anyone *but* your parents. And that's why we told them we were them."

"So, just tell the truth," Eva said.

Davey weighed in. "Mama says to always tell the truth."

"Mama is right," Angeline said. She looked at Brody. "They need to know."

"No. They really don't. But we've gotta move now."

Angeline crouched in front of Eva. "I know this is probably scary for you and your brother. But it's very important that we leave quickly."

Eva's arms tightened around her brother. "My mom and dad are in trouble, aren't they. That's why you're here."

"They're going to be fine," Brody said with enough calm assurance that even Angeline felt inclined to believe him. "But they need us to get you to a safer place than here."

Eva's eyes widened. "But—"

"We'll talk more on the way," Angeline promised. She ran her hand down the girl's arm. "For now, though, we need to listen to Brody."

"We're not s'posed to talk to strangers," Davey whispered loudly.

"Right," Angeline said quickly. "And you remember that. But we're not quite strangers, are we? Your—your mom and dad, they told us what to tell you so you'd know that."

"Falling waters," Davey said. "'Cause they al-ays wanna take us to see Angel Falls." He named the world's tallest waterfall.

"I think we should stay here," Eva said warily. "With the sisters. Then—"

"We need to get off the mountain before morning," Brody said quietly. "Which means we have to go now. Right now."

A very large tear slowly rolled down Eva's cheek. "They're dead, aren't they. They fell off the mountain they were climbing or something."

"Oh, honey. No." Angeline shook her head. "Of course not."

Brody muffled an oath and suddenly plucked Davey off Eva's lap. The boy went even wider-eyed. "Think of this as an adventure," he told the child. "You can be Peter Pan. He was always my favorite. Had his sword. Could even fly."

Angeline knew that Brody's cases usually involved children, but she was nevertheless surprised with the competent way he began stuffing the boy's feet into socks and boots as he began extolling the exciting virtues of Pan as if he really had been his favorite.

And Davey was soaking it all up like a sponge.

"They're not dead?" Eva's voice was choked.

Angeline couldn't help herself. She pulled the girl close, hugging her. "Of course not."

Another set of bells began ringing, and they both jerked, startled at the sound. "That's the four o'clock bell," Eva said. "The sisters will get up for prayers before they fix breakfast."

Brody's eyes met Angeline's. He dropped a piece of paper on Eva's vacated bed. "Just get her boots on," he muttered. "And hurry up about it."

Angeline quickly helped Eva pull on the boots. Then she tugged the sweatshirt Brody tossed her over the girl's head, right on top of the long flannel nightie.

"She's a funny looking Tinkerbell," Davey said, giggling.

Angeline figured that was much better than crying.

Brody tossed the bulging pillowcase to Angeline, blew out the candle and opened the door, cautiously looking out. A moment later, they were hurrying down the hall.

The bells fell silent and almost simultaneously, a dozen doors along the corridor opened.

Angeline held her breath and Brody muttered an oath.

No *wonder* he'd taken such a circuitous route to the children's room.

It was smack in the middle of nun central.

"You said a bad word," Davey piped out clearly.

And Brody said quite a few more as he grabbed Eva off her feet, too. Angeline ran after him as they disappeared down the narrow back staircase and out into the drizzle before any of the nuns spotted them.

Chapter Five

The "interesting collection" of vehicles evidently included a Hummer.

Stalwart and sturdy looking where it sat parked on the other side of the garden.

And though Angeline kept expecting someone to come racing after them across the wet grass, taking them to task for not waiting for the Mother Superior's all clear, no one did.

She supposed that Brody didn't waste time on such concerns. He certainly didn't waste time on manners when they reached the vehicle. He dumped the kids inside through the rear door leaving Angeline to manage for herself, and he had the engine running by the time she made it around to the passenger's side.

"Buckle up." He didn't wait to make sure they obeyed before he put the vehicle in gear and slid around in an uneven circle.

"Hold on," he warned, heading straight for a stand of bushes. "This ain't gonna be a smooth ride."

"That's an understatement," Angeline gasped moments later as the vehicle began rocking violently downward. Her head banged the window beside her, and she couldn't tell if they were on the road or not.

Another sharp drop and both Davey and Eva cried out. "We're flying," Davey hooted. "And we don't got no pixie dust even!"

"Seems like it," Brody agreed.

Angeline closed her eyes.

"What're you praying?" Brody's voice was almost as exhilarated as Davey's, and he didn't have the excuse of being four years old and innocent.

"I'm asking forgiveness for *borrowing* this vehicle and…and…oh—!" her head knocked the side window again "—and taking the kids the way we did."

"I left the sisters a note. I said someone from All-Med would return the vehicle."

Angeline gaped at him. Now he was pulling the volunteer crew in on this? "But, but that means we'll have to stop in Puerto Grande."

"Just long enough for you to fill in Dr. Chavez about getting the truck back to the convent. Believe me, we won't be staying long, and we won't be doing any rounds of visiting. There's no guarantee that our pal Rico won't have ears around."

"What if Miguel doesn't *want* to help? You know, he and the team are plenty busy without—"

"He will."

If only *she* felt as much certainty as Brody exhibited oh so easily. A tree branch slapped against the windshield and she winced. The windshield wipers were slapping away as much flying mud as rain as they hurtled down the mountain.

He'd said he wanted to get the children out of Venezuela. That wasn't going to happen on foot. "If, um, we leave the Hummer in Puerto Grande, what are we going to use as transportation then?"

"Miguel's got an SUV, doesn't he?"

She frowned. "*All-Med* has an SUV."

"And Miguel Chavez—" he broke off, cursing under his breath as they began sliding sideways. He spun the wheel, the vehicle jerked, smacked another bush straight on and continued downward again. "Like I was saying, Miguel Chavez is the head of All-Med's team. Same difference."

Not exactly. All-Med had a dozen teams that were assigned a dozen different locations.

"You're making my head hurt," she muttered.

He just grinned, and they continued bucking their way over the treacherous terrain.

The sky had begun to lighten when she finally saw from a distance their Jeep. The river of mud had climbed even higher since they'd abandoned it, and the empty vehicle listed to one side.

She swallowed a wave of nausea. If they had tried to walk back to Puerto Grande as she'd wanted, they'd have been on the road that was now fully flooded.

"Guess we won't be going that way," Brody said, clearly seeing the same thing she was.

"And neither will the Reverend Mother,"

Angeline pointed out. "There's no way she and her *guide* could get up the road again."

"I imagine a creative person would find a means," he countered.

Goodness knows Brody had.

Nothing like the creativity of *stealing* a Hummer from a bunch of nuns.

She pressed her fingertips to her eyes.

What she wouldn't give to be sitting in a coffee shop about now, doing her *regular* kind of work for Hollins-Winword.

But no, she'd had to spend her two weeks of vacation pulling another stint with All-Med.

"How'd you even find me in Puerto Grande?"

Brody had turned away from the teeming mud flow and, if her sense of direction hadn't gone completely out the window, was heading west, away from the river where the village was located.

"I told you, babe. The agency keeps track of its assets."

Right. He had. She pinched the bridge of her nose, willing away the pain that was centered there.

"You were the closest one they could find for me in a pinch," he added. His lips twitched. "Bet it makes you want to sing for joy, doesn't it?"

She wondered what he'd have done if the nearest Hollins-Winword agent had been a grizzly-looking man. Probably have come up with some other impossible plan.

"You didn't tell us why we have to go somewhere safer," Eva reminded.

The pain in Angeline's head just got worse. She lifted her brows when Brody gave her a look, as if she ought to answer. "You're the expert in these situations."

He looked about as thrilled as she felt.

But he pulled the vehicle to a stop and slung his arm over the seat, looking back at the children. "Because there's a guy—not a nice one—who wants something from your parents and *they* wanted to make sure he didn't come bothering you two at the convent before they could get back. So they asked for us to help them."

Eva swallowed. "What does he want?"

"Some of your dad's research. But that's not going to happen. So all you two need to do is stick with us. We're going to go back to the United States, and then your parents will come to meet you there. But until then, that whole talking to strangers thing? That still goes. Got it?"

Looking scared out of her wits, the girl nodded.

Davey tugged at Eva's arm, whispering something in her ear. "He has to go to the bathroom," she relayed.

Brody raked his fingers through his hair. "Anyone else?"

Eva shook her head.

Angeline felt her face flush a little as Brody looked to her. "No."

"All right, then." Leaving the vehicle running, he climbed out and opened the back door for Davey. "Us men, we got it easy," he said to the boy, who looked pretty amazed at being referred to as a man.

Eva didn't speak until after Brody closed the door and headed away with Davey. "Are you guys married?"

"What?" Angeline looked back at Eva, surprised. The wedding ring on her finger seemed to grow warm. "Oh. No. No, no. We just…work together."

Eva plucked at the nightgown hanging down below her sweatshirt. "The rain got me all wet."

"We'll get you both dried and changed when we stop in Puerto Grande." She hoped that wasn't another promise she might not be able to back up. "It looked like Brody grabbed plenty of your clothing."

"I think he's nice."

Angeline pressed her lips together and she watched Brody lead young Davey off to the side out of their eyesight. "Yes," she said after a moment. "I think you might be right."

Getting to Puerto Grande proved almost as harrowing as getting off the convent's mountain. Particularly when the rain picked up again, gaining almost as much force as it had shown the previous day.

Washed out as it was, they couldn't take the main road. So Brody put the Hummer through some severe paces, carving out their own road, until finally, what seemed hours later, they came upon the small village.

It was comprised mostly of thatched huts, some stilted, clustered along a riverside that was lush with vegetation.

Right now, the trees and bushes were swaying madly in the wind, while the river pushed well beyond its banks.

Angeline felt numb surveying the damage as Brody plowed the vehicle through the mud, keeping to higher ground as much as he could in order to reach the shack that All-Med was using.

When they finally made it, Brody pulled to a stop beside an SUV parked behind the shack. The vehicle was covered in mud and was considerably smaller than the one they'd appropriated from the nuns. "If it weren't pouring, I'd have had you leave me with the kids back by the river while you finagled Chavez out of his SUV. Now we're going to have to chance someone seeing the kids."

Angeline still didn't know how she was going to explain the situation to Miguel. She held none of Brody's confidence that the doctor who headed the team would simply hand over his keys to her. He'd been unhappy enough when she'd abandoned the camp the day before.

"You'd better get moving," Brody suggested blandly. "Just tell the guy you've still got an emergency in Caracas, but you need to borrow his truck to get you there."

"Sure. Make it sound easy." She pushed open the door and ducking her head against the rain, jogged across the rutted ground toward the shack.

She untied the flap of heavy canvas that served as a door and dashed her long sleeve over her forehead before slipping inside, refastening the flap after her.

The shack had three rooms, shotgun style, that not only served as All-Med's temporary clinic, but their sleeping quarters, as well, and she headed through to the very rear section.

"Hey there," she greeted, striving for nonchalance and surely failing miserably. "Look what the wind blew in."

Obviously startled by her appearance, Robert Smythe dropped the cards he was dealing at an ancient folding table. Maria Chavez hopped up from the folding chair on the other side of the table. "Angel! Good heavens, girl, you look like you've been swimming in the river. You and your friend surely haven't made it to Caracas and back, already?"

Along with her doctor husband, Miguel, Maria was in charge of the team. She was lithe and dark haired with skin the color of cream and caramel and with a decade on Angeline in years, she could have been an even closer "double" for Sophia Stanley.

"No. The storm stopped us." She smiled faintly at the thin blond girl who made up the third at the table. The replacement Brody had promised?

"Did you at least have some shelter last night?" Maria asked.

"Yeah." Hoping that her lies weren't too transparent, she busied herself with the pile of linens that were stacked on one of the upturned milk crates and picked a towel from the stack. "A local family—I didn't know them—took us in for the night. We, um, we borrowed their truck to get back here."

Maria looked past Angeline, as if she expected to see the man who Angeline had left with the day before.

"Brody's waiting for me in the truck," Angeline said quickly, only to wish that she'd come up with some other name for him.

Evidently, his paranoia was rubbing off on her.

She wrapped the towel around her shoulders and flipped her hair over the top of it. "It's pretty wet out there. Wet enough to keep the visitors away, I see." They'd seen at least a hundred villages despite the weather before Angeline had gone off with Brody.

"A lot of them are heading inland for higher ground." Robert deftly gathered together the cards again. "Should probably introduce you to Persia." He nodded toward the blonde. "She arrived yesterday evening."

Definitely the replacement that Brody had promised. Was this slip of a girl another Hollins-Winword asset? The newcomer looked as if she weren't even out of her teens.

She crossed the room, her hand out. "Angeline Clay. Nice to meet you."

The girl's handshake was firm. "Persia Newman. I was sorry to hear about your friend's accident. I assume you came back to pick up your stuff?" Persia's gaze stayed steady on Angeline's face.

"Uh, yes. Right. My stuff."

The girl nodded. "I thought so. I hope you don't mind, but since I was using your cot, anyway, I took the liberty of packing up your duffel. You know. Just in case you had to grab it and run."

"Miguel thought we'd maybe have to try running it up to you in Caracas," Maria added. "You'll certainly need your passport along the way."

They were so helpful that Angeline wanted

to crawl through the wood floor. "Thanks." She watched Persia move into the center room that housed the cots that made up their sleeping quarters. "So, Maria, what's the plan for the team? Are you still going to head for Los Llanos when you're finished here?"

Maria shook her head. "The plains are flooding too badly. We hear most of the roads are already underwater. Instead, we'll work our way along the coast until we end up in Puerto La Cruz." She named the popular tourist hub. "After that, we'll wait for All-Med to determine where we're best needed. This storm is going to cause some major damage, I fear." She lifted her hand. "But you don't worry about that. You just get yourself to Caracas and tend to your friend there."

Angeline moistened her lips and swallowed. Maria and Miguel and the rest were *used* to rolling with the punches and she had to think about the safety of the Stanley family. But that didn't make lying to this woman whom she considered a friend any easier. "Yes, well. About that."

Persia returned with Angeline's battered blue duffel bag. "You're good to go. Passport is in the zippered pocket inside."

"Thanks."

"How are you even getting there?"

Young she might be, but Persia Newman was definitely better at subterfuge than Angeline was. "Actually, that's another reason we came back. The, um, vehicle we borrowed belongs to the convent at St. Agnes."

Maria's eyebrows shot up. "How on earth did you get it?"

"The family we stayed with last night. Anyway, we—Brody and I—" she almost winced at saying his name yet again "—said we'd try to see that it gets returned for them to the convent, so they wouldn't have to do it themselves."

"Robert and I could drive it there," Persia offered, looking impossibly enthusiastic. "Once the weather clears a little, that is." She looked toward Maria. "You and the doctor could spare us for a few hours, right?"

"Of course." Maria readily agreed. "But that still doesn't solve Angeline's problem of getting to Caracas."

"She will take the Rover, of course." Miguel, himself, walked into the room, dashing his hand over his wet, black hair. "I was out visiting the Zamoras. They even sold their Jeep, evidently, to add to Brisa's college fund." He didn't skip a beat, jumping back to his original topic. "The keys are already in it, as usual. The Rover, that is. Why didn't you tell me that your emergency was so serious?"

"I—"

"I saw your friend, Brody, waiting outside. He told me your college friend in Caracas may not survive." Miguel dropped his hand on Angeline's shoulder. "We will all pray for her, *niña.*"

Miguel had seen Brody, obviously.

But what about the children? It didn't seem as if he'd seen *them.*

"Here." Persia pushed the duffel into Angeline's hands, as well as a canvas bag of food. "You'll need something to eat along the way."

Angeline eyed the loaves of bread, fresh fruit and the tall steel thermos that filled the bag. It just reminded her that it had been quite some time since she'd supped with Brody the night before. "But what will you guys do without the Rover?"

Manuel smiled easily. "You just leave the Rover at the All-Med office in Caracas. They'll arrange to get it back to us."

"I—I don't know what to say. Thank you."

"Angeline."

She whirled. Brody stood just inside the canvas flap. "Yes?"

"We should hurry."

"Yes." Maria began pushing Angeline toward the front of the shack where Brody waited. "We will work together again, my friend. For now, you take care of what you need."

She returned Maria's fast hug, handed back the towel and once again found herself dashing through the rain, Brody by her side.

It was beginning to feel oddly comfortable.

Chapter Six

The kids, it turned out, had been stowed by Brody out of sight inside the Rover before he'd approached the shack. Now, Eva and Davey stayed huddled down beneath a blanket as Brody took the wheel and headed away, and they didn't come out until they'd left the village of Puerto Grande entirely behind.

Brody didn't worry about finding an out-of-the-way route to Caracas. The weather was so awful that there was hardly any other traffic for them to encounter anyway, so he kept to one of the main—marginally safer—roads as they headed north.

In the backseat, Eva and Davey managed to change into some of the dry clothes that Brody had brought. Then Angeline divvied out the food, and they all took turns drinking the hot soup that filled the thermos.

And showing the resilience of youth, it was only a few hours before Eva and Davey were hunched against each other in the backseat, sound asleep.

"You should sleep, too," Brody told her when he handed her back the empty thermos lid that they'd used as a cup. She'd already tipped the last of the soup into it, assuring him that he should finish it off.

"You had even less sleep last night than I did." She was tired, but her nerves were still in such high gear that she couldn't have slept if her life depended on it. "I'm used to short nights, anyway."

"Work the late shift in Atlanta a lot?"

She tilted her head back against the headrest. "I'm surprised you don't already know."

He slanted her a look. "Turns out there are a *few* things I didn't know about you."

Her cheeks warmed. Naturally he wasn't

going to let her forget his discovery the night before.

That would hardly be Brody's style.

Of course, she hadn't thought it would be his style to play the Peter Pan card in order to keep a little boy from becoming too frightened, either.

"So, talk to me." Brody's attention was square on the road ahead of them once again. "Keep me awake, because that soup is trying to do a number on me."

"Talk about what?" she asked warily.

"Anything. What took you to Georgia in the first place."

She folded her hands together in her lap, surprised even more by his unexpected retreat from a topic that could have given him plenty of entertainment.

She wasn't ashamed of her virginity, but at her age it wasn't necessarily something she felt the need to explain, and she definitely didn't like it being the subject of amusement for someone.

"J.D. moved there first, actually," she said, not bothering to explain that J.D. was her sister when he undoubtedly already knew.

"She's the horsey one. And your brother, Casey, is the bookworm."

Despite herself, she felt a smile tug at her lips at the aptly brief descriptions. Neither sibling was hers by blood, but that hadn't kept her and J.D. from being thick as thieves. The two of them were as different as night and day, and she wasn't only Angeline's sister, she was her best friend. "Casey's finishing his graduate degree in literature—and women," she added wryly. "And J.D. is a trainer on a horse farm in Georgia."

"But she trains Thoroughbreds for racing. Kind of a departure from the whole cattle-herding thing your family does in Wyoming, isn't it?"

"She could train cutting horses just as happily. Doesn't matter to J.D., as long as she's got her beloved equines. Anyway, I followed her to Atlanta about a year after she went there."

"You were already an EMT."

She nodded. "In Casper. I got my paramedic license in Atlanta, though." She worked long hours, and when she wasn't, she was studying, taking other classes, and generally trying to decide just what she ought to be doing with her life.

"I imagine Atlanta is a whole different ball game in the medical emergency biz."

"Busier, maybe," Angeline said smoothly. She didn't really want to talk about her work. One of the reasons she'd chosen to spend her vacation time with All-Med was to get entirely away from it.

"So what are you *not* saying?"

"I don't know what you mean," she lied. Since he'd found her in Puerto Grande, she'd been doing a lot of that.

She pushed back her hair, only to have her fingers get caught in the tangles. Nothing like a reminder that she probably looked like the Wicked Witch of the West. And she couldn't easily reach her duffel at the moment where, presumably, Persia had packed her meager toiletries, because Brody had stowed it in the very rear of the vehicle.

"Yeah, right," he drawled. "Fine. Keep it to yourself. For now."

Her fingers were useless with her hair. "What are we going to do once we get to Caracas?" Focusing on the situation at hand was infinitely more appealing than thinking about Atlanta.

"We're going to get out of the country as unnoticeably as we can."

"By flying? Aside from the storm, which I would think would make that sort of difficult, we don't even have the kids' passports." She certainly hadn't noticed him adding the items when he'd filled the pillowcase with the kids' clothing.

"Yes, we do," he corrected smoothly. "I...appropriated them when I found that satellite phone. They were stored in the desk there."

She had an instant image of him rifling through the Mother Superior's desk and wondered what sort of karmic punishment *that* would deserve.

Endless rain upon an entire country?

"But it doesn't matter," he went on, oblivious to her thoughts. "Can't use them through customs anyway, because our movements could be traced. At this point we can only hope the sisters at St. Agnes bought our charade. Otherwise they could report us for taking the kids just as much as they could for us borrowing the Hummer. And even if *they* don't send up a hue and cry, it's damn sure that Rico will be watching for any sight of them when he realizes they're *not* at the convent. Which means using the international airport is not even a consideration."

"So we're going to leave the country illegally."

"Creatively," he countered. "Don't let it shock that good-girl head of yours too badly. We're not doing anything immoral. It's not as if we're running drugs or something."

She knew that. But still…. "It just seems like Hollins-Winword should be able to find more official means to get us back to the States."

The corner of his lips lifted and she realized with a start that she was actually beginning to get used to his beard and mustache. "I thought it was only your cousin Sarah who was naive about Hollins-Winword."

"Sarah's not naive," she defended. Her cousin had one of the kindest hearts she knew and was, first and foremost, an elementary school teacher. Learning last November that she'd also been pulling a stint with Hollins-Winword had come as a big surprise. Angeline had been hard pressed not to let slip what *her* work with them involved.

Her family already worried enough about her and J.D. off in Atlanta and away from the bosom of Wyoming. Add into that her cousin

Ryan who was in the Navy and had been missing now for the better part of a year, and the Clays had way more than enough concerns. She wanted to add to that with the truth about her courier sideline about as much as she wanted to beat herself with a stick.

As it was, she was hoping that this current insanity with Brody would be resolved before her vacation was up.

Nobody back home would ever be the wiser.

Brody was snorting softly. "Sarah might set up safe houses now and then, but she definitely puts a kinder face on the powers that be than I would."

Angeline pulled the last apple out of the canvas bag. "Considering that it was those same 'powers that be' who have helped to arrange her and Max adopting Megan—the girl *you* were protecting in Weaver last November—I'd have to say that my cousin seems more on the mark than you."

He'd pulled out a pocket knife earlier so she could use it to cut the apples for the kids, and she flipped the wicked blade open again, deftly slicing the fruit in quarters.

"Yeah, well, said powers don't make a habit of it." His voice went flat.

She leaned across the narrow console separating their seats and held a piece of apple up for him.

Instead of taking it from her fingers, though, he just leaned forward and grabbed it with his strong white teeth, biting off half.

She swallowed and sat back in her seat, the remaining wedge of apple still in her fingers. "We, uh, we're just going to have to agree to disagree. If it weren't for Hollins-Winword and Coleman Black, in particular—" she named the man who'd been at the helm of the underground agency for as long as she'd been alive "—I would have grown up in a Costa Rican orphanage. Instead, I ended up with Dan and Maggie. They were able to adopt me, and I even received citizenship without having to go through the usual channels."

He had an odd expression as he finished the apple piece. One she couldn't possibly hope to read. She fed him the second half, all the while trying to pretend that doing so wasn't sending odd frissons down her nerve endings.

"He was there when Santo Marguerite fell," Brody said abruptly when he'd polished off the second bite.

He referred to her father, Daniel Clay. "I

know." He'd been assigned there by none other than Coleman Black. She knew there wasn't a day that passed that he hadn't felt the weight of responsibility for being unable to prevent Sandoval's destruction there. "He's my father. Of course he told me."

"Just don't expect every situation to come up blooming the same kind of daisies."

She swallowed, instinctively looking back at the sleeping children. "Hollins-Winword operations are usually successful," she said.

"You telling me or asking me?" He shot her one of those disturbingly perceptive looks of his.

She looked away from it, focusing on the apple again. She cut another smaller wedge and leaned over, feeding it to him.

Even *that* was easier than feeling like he'd just taken a tiptoe through every fear she possessed.

When there was nothing left but the apple core, she opened the window just enough to toss it out.

"Littering." Brody shook his head, tsking and sounding more like his normal self again. "You're turning into a regular rebel."

She flicked the rainwater that had blown in

at him and told herself that she really did *not* find her insides jigging around a little at the sight of the dimple that showed, despite his disreputable whiskers.

After wiping the knife blade, she folded it again and set it back in one of the cup holders molded into the center console.

She was well aware of the periodic looks that Brody gave to the rearview and side view mirrors.

As if he expected someone to be following them.

But every time she looked back, she saw only empty road.

"Why keep pulling EMT hours when you could make more with a helluva lot less effort by focusing just on Hollins?"

"Being a courier works only because I'm able to fit it *into* my regular life. I don't want it to *become* my regular life." She lifted her hand, trying to encompass everything—the muddy vehicle, the treacherous weather, the children. "Who wants this kind of thing to be their entire life?" She shook her head, dropping her hand back to her lap. "Not me."

"I'll let the dig you just gave me pass," he said drily.

"I didn't mean—"

"Forget it." He reached up and adjusted the rearview mirror. "The truth is, my life isn't too many people's cup of java. And me, hell, I'd be bored stiff if I had to stay in any one place for too long a stretch. But I didn't mean that you should try to be in the field all the time. Just that you could be kept a lot busier as a courier than you are, if you wanted."

She shook her head. "I don't."

"Smart girl," he murmured almost as if to himself. Then he shot her a look. "As a source of excitement, your job probably gives plenty, right?"

Her fingers strayed to the tangles in her hair again. "I suppose." She'd dealt with everything from delivering babies to people who'd died peacefully in their sleep. And most everything in between.

She knew what it felt like to lose a battle that she couldn't have won no matter what, and that was fine. She still slept at night.

It was the battle that she hadn't *had* to lose that plagued her. The one where she'd hesitated, where she'd made the wrong choice, taken the wrong action. That was the thing she wasn't able to accept. The thing that made her question pretty much everything she'd thought she wanted to do with her life.

Supposedly, knowing any problem—identifying it, putting a name to it—was supposed to be the first step in dealing with it.

So far, the theory hadn't helped her one iota.

She'd still let a fourteen-year-old kid down, in the most final of ways because she'd thought she could get to him without having to climb through a culvert.

Brody flicked the windshield wipers to a higher setting. They swished back and forth so rapidly, they were almost nothing but a blur of motion. He checked the rearview again.

Angeline looked back through the window. All she could see was the misty swirl of water kicked up by the tires as it warred with the rain. "You don't think we're being followed, do you?" The notion tasted acrid.

"No."

She turned forward once more and chewed on her lower lip for a moment. "Are you lying?"

"I've always thought that one of those useless no-win questions." His voice was considering.

She folded her arms. "Well, pardon me."

"Seriously, think about it." His thumb lifted off the steering wheel. "If a person *is* lying, they're hardly going to want to admit it. If they say they're not, why is that anymore believable than the original lie? And no matter whether they ever admit that they are lying, the person who asked the question in the first place is going to be no happier knowing it. Because they either want to believe what the person did say or they don't."

She squinted at him. "I'm sorry. Was that supposed to make *any* sense?"

He shrugged.

She propped her elbow on the door and covered her eyes with her hands. "Davey's the one who had it right, anyway. It's just better to tell the truth."

"Maybe in a perfect world." He gave her a look. "This ain't a perfect world, Angeline. The sooner you face that, the better off you'll be."

Angeline.

So he *could* manage her name when he felt like it.

Unfortunately, she now knew—too late of

course—that hearing her name roll off his lips was far more disturbing to her peace of mind.

Once they reached Caracas, even with the aid of the city map Angeline found in the glove box, it took two efforts before she was able to direct Brody through the confusing streets to the All-Med office. Naturally, when they got there, the small storefront was locked up tight for the night.

When Brody strolled past, speculatively studying the assortment of vehicles parked on the street, Angeline was too tired to muster any surprise. "Nobody's going to be at the office until tomorrow morning to do anything about returning this thing to Miguel. Don't you think we might as well keep driving it until then? The kids need to eat, Brody. You and I need to eat. And a shower and some fresh clothes wouldn't necessarily hurt any of us, either."

"How much cash do you have?"

"Not much. Just what I had back at the camp in Puerto Grande. I don't carry a lot cash when I come here; it's easier to use my credit card."

"Can't use that."

She wasn't surprised. Electronic means were too easily traced.

In the rear, Davey was pushing at Eva, complaining that she was hogging too much of the seat. Angeline reached her hand back, automatically trying to separate them. "You two have been great all day today, and I know you're tired. But just have patience for a little while longer," she urged.

Brody raked his hand down his face. "We've already stayed with this SUV too long."

Angeline swallowed. The reality of their situation had hovered beneath the surface throughout the long day of driving. Now it gurgled again to the surface like some dank, oily monster. But throwing up her hands in panic wasn't going to solve anything.

The children still needed food and some chance to stretch their legs before they got some sleep in a proper bed.

Brody turned on the interior light and pulled the map across the steering wheel. "Do you know this area?" he asked pointing to a spot.

Angeline shook her head. "I don't know much of Caracas at all, except the airport and how to get from there to the All-Med office."

Eva sat forward, poking her head between

the seats. "Tell Davey to stop kicking me or I'm gonna *punch* him."

"Nobody is going to kick or punch *anyone,*" Angeline said, giving them both a firm look.

Brody pushed the map back toward Angeline, turned off the overhead light and began driving up the narrow street. "We'll find a place to hole up for the night, and get you settled with the kids. Once that's done, I'll ditch the SUV back at All-Med."

Somehow she doubted that he'd be catching a taxi back to the hotel after he'd done so. But she didn't want to delve too deeply into what alternative means he'd likely use.

This time, when it seemed as if they were driving around the city in circles, it wasn't because she'd told him to turn the wrong direction toward All-Med. It was because he was doing it deliberately.

Just in case. The realization was sobering.

Then finally, *finally,* he pulled up to a non-descript hotel that seemed as if it was located about as far from All-Med's office as it could be.

"Amazing," he murmured. "This place is

still here." He shot her a quick look. "Stay here. Keep the doors locked. This place is no St. Agnes."

She pressed her lips together. She was perfectly aware that many of the cheap hotels were more in the business of renting by the hour than playing home base for vacationing families. Judging by the few people she saw milling around, she suspected that the hourly rate probably wasn't all that high, either.

"I don't like this place," Eva said once Brody disappeared into the building.

"Neither do I," Angeline murmured. "But it might be the best we can do in a pinch. And Brody will make sure we're safe."

"Are you sure?"

Was she?

She swallowed, ready to offer the lie that would keep the girl from worrying any more than she already was.

But then she saw Brody heading back toward them, his stride long and purposeful. The lamppost nearby cast a circle of light over him, highlighting the sparkle of raindrops catching in his disheveled hair.

A curious calm centered inside her.

"Yes, Eva, I'm sure."

There wasn't an ounce of untruth in her words.

Chapter Seven

"Here." Brody tossed the oversized room key into Angeline's lap as he climbed behind the wheel once more. He was becoming heartily sick of the rain. "It's a room in the very back. Supposed to be more...quiet than some."

She held the key between her long fingers. "You seem familiar with the place. Have you stayed here before?"

"No."

She lifted her eyebrows, clearly expecting more of an explanation.

He was more interested in getting rid of the

All-Med vehicle as quickly and thoroughly as possible than he was in satisfying Angeline's curiosity over his sometimes misspent years.

He drove the truck around to the far back side of the building. Habit had him cataloging not only the people loitering about but also the vehicles parked there, as well.

He parked, and took the key back from Angeline. "Let me check the room."

"More paranoia?"

"Paranoia keeps me sane, baby cakes." He opened the door, hit the door locks to lock them in again, and crossed the laughable excuse of a sidewalk to room number twenty-nine.

The interior wasn't going to win any awards, but it looked cleaner than he'd expected. The two beds appeared marginally adequate. Unfortunately, both had mirrors mounted on the ceilings above them, but they weren't in a position to be finicky. There was also a television, a couple of chairs and a bathroom.

He stepped into the doorway, gesturing for Angeline and the kids.

Neither Davey nor Eva wasted any time.

They raced into the room, jockeying for first dibs on the bathroom.

Eva won.

Brody chucked Davey under the chin as he morosely stomped away from the door that his sister had shut in his face. "Get used to it, son. Girls *always* get dibs on the loo."

Angeline dropped the kids' pillowcase on the table. "Sounds like you speak the voice of experience."

"What's a loo?"

"A bathroom," Angeline told Davey when Brody didn't answer.

Dragging his thoughts away from the experience he *had* once had was difficult. Too difficult.

He must be more tired than he thought. Why the hell else would he keep thinking about Penny? About things that had occurred decades before?

His sister was dead.

Just like the rest of his family.

He didn't let himself think at all about the man who'd taken him in after that. Not when he blamed him for all of it in the first place.

Angeline was walking back and forth in front of him and the boy, evidently well into female mode as she clucked over the ceiling mirrors that Davey had just discovered and seemed fascinated by.

Wondering what kind of thoughts filled Angeline's head about the presence of the mirrors was enough, at least, to help Brody close the door on the past again.

When she noticed him watching her, dusky color filled her cheeks and she quite obviously turned her attention to the thin spreads on the bed, the pillows, the metal hangers hanging in the cupboard. Not even the surface of the dresser missed her examination.

"Sorry I don't have a white glove handy," he drawled.

Angeline pursed her lips together, and she'd probably have been appalled that the look didn't really have the intended effect on him. He didn't exactly feel taken to task when he was more interested in exploring the faint dimple that appeared, just below the corner of those smooth, full, pressed-together lips.

Flirting with Angeline was one thing. She was eminently flirtworthy. The perfect mark: a combination of smarts and wit and innocence—hell, he'd never be able to forget just *how* innocent after he'd stepped onto that particular buried mine—that combined together in one impossibly appealing package.

Fortunately, Eva opened the bathroom door then, ensuring that Brody—plagued with unwanted memories and inconvenient desires—didn't do something really stupid.

The young girl barely had time to get out of the way as Davey bolted inside.

The clothes that Eva had changed into in the SUV all those hours ago were mismatched and wrinkled, and he wasn't all that surprised when she hugged her arms around her thin body, giving wary looks to both him and Angeline, who was now busy trying to make some order out of the pillowcase contents. Eva sidled around the room to sit in one of the chairs near the small window next to the door.

The long ride after their precipitous exit from St. Agnes and then Puerto Grande had lulled her into a quiet acceptance of the situation. But now, her Stanley mind was probably ticking furiously away over everything that had occurred.

Angeline sighed, and pushed nearly all of the newly folded clothing neatly back into the pillowcase. It looked to him like what she'd left out was for the following day. Then she turned and folded her arms over her chest.

She, like he, hadn't had the advantage of changing out of the tunic and pants the nuns had provided and he wondered if she was as aware as he just how thin the linen really was as it closely draped her magnificent curves.

"You didn't manage to grab any pajamas," she told Brody.

He shrugged. That was the least of their worries. "That's what T-shirts are for," he dismissed.

She accepted it without argument.

Which only made his stupid brain drift on down the dangerous avenue of wondering just what Angeline usually wore to bed.

T-shirts?

Little silky nightgowns?

Nothing at all?

He scrubbed his hand down his face. He'd be better off envisioning her in thick flannel from head to toe, but suspected that even that wouldn't derail him. "Food," he said abruptly. "I'm gonna go scavenge up some food for everyone."

Eva couldn't hide the relief on her young face at that idea and Brody felt a pang inside.

He'd pushed hard all that day and the kids had been troopers. Angeline, too, for that matter.

But they weren't used to being on the run.

He went to the door, opened it enough to look through the crack, then stepped out. "Angeline."

She joined him.

He pulled her farther out the door, closing it slightly so that Eva couldn't see. Being at the end of the building, he didn't worry much about being seen by any of the guys who were hanging around the hotel.

Angeline eyed him. "What is it?"

He deliberately reached out and grabbed her slender waist, pulling her until she stood less than a foot from him.

Her lips parted, startled. "Brody—"

When he lifted the hem of her tunic, her expression went frosty and she slammed her palms hard against his inner elbows.

"Relax," he muttered, even as he was sort of impressed with the strength behind the movement that had knocked his unprepared hands clean away from her all-too-lovely body.

He lowered his head toward hers, enjoying way too much how she stiffened. Whether it was pride or not that kept her from sliding a step back from him as he invaded her personal space even more, he couldn't tell.

He lifted the hem of her tunic again, drawing it right up over those curving hips. High enough to see the drawstring that held the pants—not very effectively he noticed—around her very narrow waist.

His fingers brushed against the satin-smooth plane of her belly.

She inhaled on a hiss. "What—"

"Shh," he hushed, and because he was running on no sleep, no food and clearly no smarts, he grazed his lips over hers.

Whether that shocked her more than the Glock he tucked into the front and center waist of her pants or not as he kissed her, he couldn't tell.

Fortunately though, some cells in his brain were still in functioning order, and he brusquely tugged her tunic back down in place, and stepped away. "Take care of Delilah for me."

Her hand slapped against her belly, obviously holding the weapon in place. "I don't want her. *This*."

"I don't care." He knew she was capable of shooting it, because he knew what kind of training Hollins-Winword had put her through.

Even couriers needed to know how to fire a weapon whether or not it was ever likely to be necessary.

Besides, she'd grown up on a ranch. She'd probably known way more about firearms at an early age than *he* had.

Kids born to a British barrister and a surgeon didn't have much need to be around weapons.

Or they shouldn't have had a need if Cole would have just kept his distance from Brody's mother.

"Do you really think Rico would show up here?" Angeline lifted one hand, cutting off the pointless speculation going on inside his head. He'd given up years before wondering what would have happened if anything had been different.

"You drove around in so many circles, I don't even have a clue where in the city we are," she went on. "Nobody could possibly have followed us without us noticing."

"What I hope for versus what I know is possible are two very different things. There's an extra clip in your duffel bag. The cash I've got is in there, too."

"When did you put it in there— oh, never

mind." She looked resigned. "You *are* just going out to get us some food, right?"

"Now, I am. Consider this a run through for when I take the SUV back to All-Med."

"When will that be?"

"Later. The point is, you have to be prepared for anything, Angeline."

She moistened her lips. He saw the swallow she made work its way down her long, lovely throat. "O-okay."

"If I'm not back by dawn—that's *if*," he emphasized when she looked startled, "I want you to go back to the office here, talk to Paloma. She said she'll still be working even in the morning. She used to be sort of trustworthy—"

"*Used* to be?" Her fingers closed over his wrists, only to let go again, to press against her waistband. "I'm really not liking the sound of this."

"Yeah, well, beggars can't be choosers. Necessity is the mother of invent— Hell." He dropped the light tone. "Just listen. She'll get you to a guy who can get you all to Puerto Rico."

"But what about the storm? There aren't even any flights going right now."

"*Now* is not tomorrow morning. Try not to agree to a price that'll use up all the cash—but do it if you have to. Once you get to Puerto Rico, look up a hotel called Hacienda Paradise. Owner's name is Roger. Think you can remember that?"

She looked insulted. "Of course. Roger. Hacienda Paradise. Hardly complicated."

"Tell him Simon sent you."

Her eyebrows rose. "Simon?"

"Just tell him. He'll get you back into the States."

"Just on the say-so of Simon. What is that? Another one of your aliases?"

He exhaled. "Can you do that?"

"Yes, I can do that. But it's not going to be necessary. Because *you're* going to be back." Her voice lost a little tartness. "Aren't you?"

"I'm going to try like hell," he said evenly. "But even the best situations can fall apart. And, sorry to say, babe, this isn't the best of situations. If I'd had a little more time to prep the op, it would have been kind of helpful. As it is, we're sort of flying by the seat of my pants."

"Well." She tugged at her disheveled

hair. "Better your pants, than flying by someone else's."

"Babe." He pressed his hand to his heart. "I'm touched."

She exhaled suddenly, rolling her eyes, and reached for the door again to go back inside. "Just hurry up and get us some food, would you please? My stomach is about ready to eat through itself to the other side." She slipped into the room and closed the door.

He waited until he heard her slide the lock into place.

Good girl.

She's not a girl, you twit.

He ignored the voice, perfectly well aware that Angeline was entirely *all* woman.

Then he went in search of the only kind of sustenance he was going to be sharing with his beautiful, virginal partner.

By the time Brody made it back *with* food, Angeline had run the kids through baths and into their improvised pajamas—a pale green scrub top of Angeline's for Eva, and a T-shirt of Eva's for Davey. She supposed that he was just too worn-out to protest the T-shirt with the glittery princess printed on the front.

In any case, they were clean and barely keeping their eyes open as they watched the grainy television channel showing a Spanish-dubbed version of an old American sitcom, when Brody knocked on the door.

Angeline's hand went to Delilah—she couldn't believe she was thinking of the Glock like another woman—that was tucked into her pants. It had been hidden there ever since he'd tucked it in her waistband, well over an hour earlier. She peeked through the dingy orange drape hanging at the window and relief made her feel positively weak-kneed at the sight of him standing on the other side of the door.

She quickly undid the lock and opened it for him.

He pushed the large brown bag into her hands and headed for the bathroom.

"Come on, my dears. Supper time," she said cheerfully.

Davey's tiredness almost miraculously abated at the idea of food. Eva, however, just shuffled silently to the table, slipping into one of the two chairs closest to the wall.

The feast Brody had returned with turned out to be a filling one. There were red beans and rice, and some sort of pork and chicken, tortillas and several bottles of water, as well as a few cans of soda with the easily recognizable kind of logos that transcended translation and a handful of wax-paper-wrapped sweet pastries. Soon Brody joined them.

Like Angeline, he sat on one side of the bed facing the table. And he ignored the paper plate she'd left for him, instead using the foil container that had held the beans and rice as his plate.

He didn't say much of anything as he ate, and when he thanked her for the opened bottle of water she handed him, she knew something was up.

Not from the tone of his voice. Goodness, no. She could hardly ever tell anything from his voice—or not very accurately, anyway. Nor was it his expression, which was as inscrutable as it ever was. His blue eyes—she was almost positive now that they must be his natural color, because she hadn't once seen him take out or put in contact lenses since they'd stared up the mountain to St. Agnes—were unreadable.

And it certainly wasn't anything he expressed in words, which at the moment—around mouthfuls of food—tended to center on answering Davey's questions about how high did Brody think he could jump when using a mattress as a springboard.

Brody gave Angeline a quick look. "Wants to jump on the bed, does he?"

She nodded. "He wants to see his handprints on the mirror up there." It was better than if the boy had expressed too much curiosity over *why* there were mirrors on the ceiling. She hadn't let him jump on the bed, of course, but she'd still considered it a good sign that he wasn't becoming too distressed over their activities. She wished she could believe the same was true about Eva.

The girl was becoming increasingly withdrawn.

She didn't even bat an eye when Davey slid the onions he'd carefully picked out of his chicken concoction onto her paper plate or when he plucked her pastry out of its wrapper and broke a gargantuan piece from it.

"Davey," Brody said, his tone warning.

The boy's shoulders drooped. He handed the pastry back to his sister.

She just shook her head. She'd only eaten half her meal. "You can have it. I'm full, anyway." She began to push herself back from the tiny table. "Oh. May I be excused?"

"Of course." Angeline caught the thin paper napkin that had been on Eva's lap before it fell to the floor as the girl slipped out from between the table and the wall and went over to the far bed.

She climbed onto one side, and lay facedown, burying her head in the pillow.

"She just sleepy?" Brody's voice was low.

Angeline watched the prone girl for a long moment. She couldn't decide what was more worrisome—wondering what was bothering Brody that he wasn't telling her, or Eva's exhaustion. "I hope so."

"Well, sleep is what you all need," he said. He grabbed the other uneaten half of Eva's fruit-filled pastry, and polished it off in just two bites.

She began wrapping up the trash, setting aside the water and sodas they hadn't yet opened. They wouldn't go to waste because they'd definitely need them sooner or later. Brody stuffed the trash back into the sack. "I'll pitch it in the bin outside," he said.

Which only had disquiet curling through her all over again, because Brody's remaining task for the night had yet to begin.

She told Davey to wipe his hands and face

and get into the unoccupied bed. "Brody, wait." She joined him at the door.

"Planning a little segregation of the sexes tonight? Girls in one bed? Guys in the other?" His lips twitched as he lowered his head closer to hers. "They'd be good chaperones, babe, just in case you're worried that two nights in a row with me in the same bed might be more temptation than you can handle."

She felt her face heat. "Get over yourself, would you?"

He chuckled softly, but when he straightened again, his expression was serious. "Don't forget now. Palo—"

"Paloma. Roger, Hacienda Paradise. Simon. I know. I know."

He nodded and turned to go, but she put her hand on his arm, stopping him. "Something's bothering you," she said quietly. "What?"

His expression didn't change. "Nothing new."

"Right. Too bad I don't believe that." She looked over her shoulder at the children. Davey's attention was focused once more on the television set, and all she could see of Eva was the back of her head. "What happened when you went out for the food?"

"Nothing."

"And I believe that like I believe in Santa Claus."

"Well, you are as untouched as an eight-year-old," he drawled, "so it wouldn't surprise me at all to find you sitting in front of the fireplace every Christmas Eve ready to greet the jolly old dude with milk and cookies warm from your oven."

Her lips tightened. "Don't patronize me."

He sighed roughly. "There's nothing you can do about it anyway, so forget about it."

Her fingers tightened on his uncompromisingly hard arm. "Do…about…*what?*"

"I couldn't reach my handler."

She frowned a little. "So?"

He looked upward. "So. So, that's a problem."

"Because someone didn't answer a phone just once when you expected them to? Maybe he was busy."

"She."

"Fine. Maybe *she* was busy."

"Handlers don't do *busy.* They're available 24/7. Period."

She rubbed her neck. "Well, you'll just have to try again," she stated the obvious, and received a wry "you think?" look right back from him as a result.

"Getting us all back to the States is going to be a helluva lot easier with some help than without," he told her. "I'm not saying it's impossible without it. What I am saying is that it's…unusual…not to be able to reach her. Plus, no contact means no updates on the Stanleys' situation."

It was a sobering thought. "Who is your handler, anyway?" The world that Hollins-Winword operated in was often murky and ill defined. They didn't operate counter to the federal government, of course, who often found it helpful that the agency was able to move where official means were impossible. Nor did it matter if the problem was small and domestic, or invasive and international. The people involved with the agency were sometimes far-flung, and they certainly didn't operate out of any typical office building.

"You know I'm not gonna tell you," Brody was looking amused again. "No offense, babe, but that's strictly need to know."

"But what if I did need to know?" She hugged her arms to herself. "Theoretically speaking, I mean. Would you ever break *those* rules?" She was acutely aware of his propensity for breaking others.

"It's pretty obvious there are plenty of rules I'm willing to break." His gaze drifted downward, seeming to hesitate around her mouth. "But there are a few—probably too few to make much of a saint out of me—that I won't." Then he closed the door.

She swallowed, her mouth suddenly dry. She wasn't sure just exactly what they were talking about, but she feared it had nothing to do with her question about his handler.

Chapter Eight

Angeline was awake and sitting in the chair, facing the door, when the fingers of dawn light crept eerily around the edges of the ill-fitted orange window drape.

In one bed, Eva slept soundly. She hadn't stirred once all night long.

In the other bed, Davey slept, too, though he'd tossed and turned enough for both himself and his sister.

Climbing into bed, herself, was just not something she could make herself do. Not with Brody's "in case of emergency" instructions circling in her head.

Brody hadn't returned.

Which meant that, if she were a good Hollins-Winword agent, she'd get the children up and dressed and race down to the office and this Paloma whom Brody *thought* might be trustworthy.

She rubbed her eyes and the dim light just grew stronger.

Problem was, she *wasn't* a particularly good Hollins-Winword agent. She wasn't cut out for this cloak-and-dagger stuff. She was just a courier of information for them. That's all she'd *ever* been!

And he expected her to get the kids, ultimately, back to the United States and just leave him behind?

How on earth was she supposed to make herself do that?

Not even during her worst shifts in Atlanta had she felt so tired. So rattled. So unsure of herself.

It was even worse than—

The doorknob jiggled and she sat up like a shot, dragging her feet off the second chair so quickly that it tipped onto its back, bouncing softly on the threadbare carpet.

She tossed aside the bright blue towel

she'd draped over her lap and Delilah after she'd raced through her own shower, and scrambled over the chair, nearly tripping on the legs as she made for the door.

She threw open the lock and yanked open the door.

Brody stood there, looking furious. "What the *hell* are you still doing here?"

"Be quiet," she muttered, "just be quiet." And she wasn't sure who she shocked more when she reached up and wrapped her arms around his neck. "Don't *ever* scare me like that again."

His arms had come around her back. "Angel—"

"You were gone *hours!*" She squeezed his neck again. For some reason she couldn't seem to stop herself from clinging.

"Okay. Ohhh-kay." He sounded a little strangled, and his hands went from her back to unhook the ones she'd locked around his neck like some manic noose. He worked the Glock she still held out of her clenched fingers, and tucked it in the small of his back, then closed his hands around her fists and pulled them between them. "Breathe, would you?"

She drew in a huge breath, hardly aware that she'd been holding it in the first place.

"Better." He reached over her shoulder and pushed the door wider. "At least you were armed," he said gruffly. "Get inside."

She backed up as he headed forward enough that he could close the door once more. "Wake them up."

He was still furious, she realized.

And though she felt some compunction for not having followed his exact instructions, she didn't feel overly apologetic, either.

After all, he'd arrived, hadn't he?

He'd arrived, she realized belatedly, wearing a completely different set of clothing than the disheveled tunic and pants that he'd left wearing.

"You've got different clothes."

He was righting the chair that she'd tipped over. *"Now."* He was clearly not referring to her observation.

She sidled past him, heading for Eva. The girl, when she finally sat up, looked glassy-eyed and pale.

Angeline frowned a little, pressing her palm against Eva's forehead. It didn't feel overly warm, though. "Come on, sweetie, it's time for us to get moving again." She pulled over the clothing that she'd set out the night before. "Can you get yourself changed?"

Eva nodded and without argument began exchanging the scrub top for her own jeans and sweatshirt.

Brody had disappeared into the bathroom. She heard the shower come on, and made a face at the closed door. Obviously he wasn't in such a hurry that he couldn't manage a few minutes for that particular necessity.

She turned her attention to Davey. Like the previous day, he didn't wake quite as easily as his sister. But when he did, he began dressing himself, assuring Angeline quite indignantly that he did not need help.

She hadn't even finished tucking the kids' improvised nightwear back into the pillow-case when Brody came out, dressed again in the unexpected blue jeans and dark blue T-shirt. His hair was wet and slicked back from his face, and without looking at her, he picked up her small toiletry bag sitting on the edge of the chipped white sink and began rummaging through it.

"Can I help you find something?"

His gaze met hers briefly in the mirror

above the sink as he pulled out her tooth-
paste and her toothbrush and began
brushing his teeth.

She didn't know what disturbed her more.

The fact that he was using her toothbrush,
or the fact that she wasn't absolutely appalled
that he was using her toothbrush.

He was still watching her through the re-
flection of the mirror.

She swallowed and bundled up the towel
she'd been using as a lap blanket and stuck it
back inside her duffel. She pulled on her sturdy
boots again, and when she looked toward
Brody again, he'd finished brushing his teeth
and had soaped up his face with bar soap and
was stroking her narrow pink razor over his
jaw, muttering an oath with every pass.

Her eyes drifted down from the way the
T-shirt stretched tight over his shoulders to
the way it was nearly loose at his narrow
waist where it—along with the grip of the
weapon—was tucked into his jeans.

She quickly looked away again before he
could catch her ogling his undeniably *fine*
backside, and helped Davey tie his tennis
shoes.

When she was finished, Brody was wiping

the last bit of soap suds from his newly revealed jawline.

She turned her eyes from the bead of blood on his angular chin and told the kids to be sure to use the restroom before they left.

Once again, Eva—finally showing some energy—darted in first.

Davey's shoulders hunched forward and his head tilted back. "Gaaawwwwwl."

Angeline handed him the pastry that she hadn't eaten from the night before. "Maybe this'll help." She caught Brody's look. "What?" she said defensively. "It's basically a fruit Danish."

"Did I say something?"

She narrowed her eyes. "You didn't have to."

He moved toward her and dropped the toiletry bag in her hand. "Yet when I really *do* say something, you ignore it completely."

Her lips parted. "That is not fair."

His eyebrows rose. His jaw was still shiny and damp and his raked back hair looked nearly black with water. He looked like some archangel, fallen to earth.

And was mighty peeved about the entire process.

"Just how is it *not* fair, love? Did you head

out at dawn, like I told you to? Did you speak with Paloma? Did you buy your way across the water to Puerto Rico? Did you do any…single…thing…I told you to do?" His voice dropped with every word, only succeeding in making his anger even more evident. "Dammit, Angeline, I trusted you to—"

"To what?" She refused to back away, but keeping her chin up in the face of that dark, blue-eyed glower was no small feat. She was also aware of Davey's avid attention, but couldn't seem to stop her tongue. "To leave you behind?" She propped her hands on her hips. "How could you really think I could leave you behind?"

He exhaled, sounding aggravated beyond measure. "Believe me, I think I could have managed to keep my head above water, even without your help."

She sniffed imperiously, though the sarcastic words stung. Deeply. "Well, next time, I won't make the same mistake, I assure you."

"You'd better not."

She turned away and since both Eva and Davey had taken their turns with the bathroom, she stomped across the room and shut herself behind the door.

Only there did she let her shoulders relax.

She pressed her hand to her heart, willing its thunderous pounding to still, for the shudders working down her spine to cease.

But she nearly jumped out of her skin a moment later when he wrapped his knuckles on the other side of the wood panel. "Hurry it up," he told her brusquely. "We're rolling in five minutes."

She stared at the door. Stuck her tongue out at it and felt both foolish and better.

But before five minutes had passed, she'd finished the most necessary of her morning ablutions, and the four of them left the cheap hotel room behind, toting their ragtag belongings with them.

The air outside was chilly and damp; the sky above a heavy, dull gray that was turning to silver with every centimeter of sunlight that rose.

But it wasn't raining. At least not at the moment. It was one bright spot, she thought, as she took Davey's hand in hers and followed after Brody.

He did not, as she had expected, head for the office to consult with the still-unseen Paloma. Brody crossed the street, heading for the corner where he stopped beside a mustard-yellow taxicab. Despite the lack of a driver sitting behind the wheel, he pulled open the back door, tossed in Angeline's duffel that he'd evidently decided she was too inept to carry herself, and nudged Eva in after. Davey ran ahead to join his sister, and Angeline quickly broke into a jog herself.

Brody shut the door after Davey and flung open the passenger's door, then rounded to the driver's side.

She ought to have known not to be surprised by anything, but she couldn't help herself when she sat down in the front seat next to Brody. "Where's the driver?"

He shrugged. "Hopefully sleeping for another few hours so we can ditch this someplace before he even realizes it's gone."

Another stolen car.

She sank her teeth into her tongue, determined to remain silent on the matter. He *was* supposed to be the expert, here.

It was strictly her problem that she immediately had visions of the two of them being forever incarcerated in some horrible jail cell on multiple counts of grand theft auto, and kidnapping. And the children—

She couldn't think that way. As long as Brody was around, the children would be safe.

The man in question was weaving through the streets that seemed congested even at such an early hour and Angeline faced the irony in her cogitations.

She was riddled with anxiety over his disregard for legalities, yet she still trusted that he'd see them all safely through this.

But then that's the way it had always been with Brody.

Equal measures of wary fascination and instinctive trust. Both of which she'd been wise to refrain from examining too closely.

Up until now, that had been fairly easy to do, considering how rare and brief their encounters had always been.

He slammed on the brakes suddenly, throwing his arm up to keep her from falling forward.

She pressed her lips together, painfully aware of his palm pressed hard against her sternum as the car shuddered to a stop.

She imagined she could feel each centimeter of those long fingers burning a tattoo into her skin.

So much for easy.

"You okay?"

She nodded even though she was aware that it was the children he'd addressed. Assured that they were, his gaze slid over Angeline and he pulled his palm away from her chest, wrapping it once more around the steering wheel.

Ahead of them, she spotted a three-car pileup. Judging by the trio of men standing around yelling and gesturing, she was fairly certain that nobody had been hurt. At least she couldn't see anybody still inside the vehicles.

Nevertheless, she threw open her door and ran forward, hardly aware of Brody's oath behind her.

She went first to the car that had been hit on both sides, looking through the windows. A woman was lying on her side across the backseat, her hands pressed to her distended abdomen.

Angeline scrambled with the door, but it was too badly crunched to open. She knocked on the window drawing the woman's attention. "Are you hurt?" She repeated it in Spanish when the woman gave her a confused look.

"My baby is coming too fast," she replied.

Naturally. Life wasn't giving any easy outs these days. Angeline smiled encouragingly and promised to return in a moment. She ran to the other cars that were thankfully empty now and headed back to the pregnant woman, trying the opposite door this time with no better results.

Brody was storming toward the cars and she ignored him as she managed to wriggle her arm through the window of the door that seemed to have less damage, and twisted her arm around enough to roll the window down farther. She was amazed it moved at all, given the sharp dent in the door. When it was down, she ducked through, running her hands cautiously along the woman's legs which were bared by the bright red dress she wore. *"Mi nombre es Angeline,"* she told the woman calmly.

"Soledad," the woman replied around panting breaths. "The other car, it came from nowhere. My husband—"

"He's out calling for help," Angeline blithely lied the assurance. As far as she could tell, the three men weren't doing a single productive thing but yelling obscenities at each other. "How far apart are your pains?"

"Minutes."

No easy outs and hellacious innings to boot, she thought. "I'll be right back," she promised the woman, and pulled her torso back out of the window. She turned, nearly bumping into Brody, who was standing behind her, looking thoroughly maddened.

"What the bloody hell do you think you're doing?" His voice was calm. Pleasant even.

She actually felt herself start to quail. But a cry from the woman trapped in the car stiffened her resolve. "She's in labor," she told him hurriedly. "Both doors are jammed. You need to see if any one of those guys—" she threw out her arm "—has called for help."

"In case you've forgotten, we are sort of in the middle of our *own* emergency."

She lifted her hands at her sides. "Is Ri— our friend on our tail right this minute? Have you seen him?" She didn't wait for an answer. "What would you really have me do, Brody? Ignore that poor woman? Good heavens, at least *this* sort of thing I'm trained to handle!"

"Deliver a lot of babies on the side of roads do you?"

"This will be my tenth, if you must know!

Now make yourself useful and find some way to get one of those doors open." She pushed past him and hurried back to the taxi.

Eva and Davey were sitting with their arms crossed over the back of the front seat as they watched the action unfold in front of them. Angeline managed a quick look into Eva's face and felt a little better about the girl—she'd worried when she'd woken her that she might be coming down with something. But now, she looked more like her regular self again.

Angeline dragged open her duffel, rooting past the clothes and the small toiletry bag. She dragged out the blue towel again and her bottle of waterless antibacterial soap. Then, at the very bottom of the bag, she found her first-aid kit. She tucked the webbed strap of its holder over her shoulder. "Eva, can you hand me one of the water bottles?"

Eva pulled one out of her pillowcase-luggage and handed it over. "What're you doing?"

"There's a woman about to have a baby in that blue car," she said. "I'm going to help her. You two wait here in the taxi, okay?"

"Brody looks mad," Eva said.

"He's just concerned that we get you two

back to the States as quickly as possible." The last part was truthful, at least. "Hopefully, this won't take too long and we'll be doing just that before you can say Jack Sprat."

"Huh?"

She smiled and shook her head before hurrying back to the vehicle. Brody had evidently convinced the arguing parties to pool their efforts in more productive ways since two of them were leaning their weight against a crowbar, trying to work the least mangled door free.

"Wait." Angeline waved off their work for a moment. She tossed her collection of supplies through the window onto the front seat. "Help me climb inside first," she told Brody in English. "I'm worried that she's too far along to wait until you get the door jimmied."

The distinctive wail of sirens suddenly filled the air.

"Great," Brody muttered. "You're playing Nurse Nightingale and the freaking police are getting ready to join the party."

"You're the one used to adapting to the situation. Adapt." She tucked her head and torso through the window as far as she could. "You'll have to push me the rest of the way."

She'd do it herself, but she simply couldn't gain enough leverage to either pull or push herself through.

His hands circled her waist and he nudged her inches forward. She wasn't exactly a wide load, but her hips had always been more curvaceous than she'd have liked, and the window was hardly generous. She shimmied and sucked in a hard breath when Brody's hands moved from her waist to plant square against her derriere.

"Desperate situations necessitate desperate measures," he said, sounding amused as her rear cleared the window's confines and she pretty much landed on her face on the front seat.

She dragged her feet in after her. "Keep working on the door," she said, not looking at him as she maneuvered her way awkwardly into the backseat.

The woman was drenched in sweat and amniotic fluid.

Angeline smiled again as she started to draw the woman's soaked skirt upward.

"Are you a doctor?"

"Sort of." Angeline didn't hesitate. "Have you had other babies?"

The woman nodded. *"Tres."*

"Ah. Then you're an old hand at this," Angeline said brightly. She kept up a running conversation in Spanish with the woman—as much as her panting would allow at any rate—to keep her distracted from the pain. She doused her hands liberally with the anti-biotic soap, and reminded herself as she checked the woman for dilation that Miguel and Maria Chavez had delivered children with even fewer sanitary conveniences.

Soledad was not just fully dilated, the baby was already crowning.

With the sirens drawing ever nearer, Angeline reached over the seat to drag open her meager medical kit. She had a few packages of sterile gloves but didn't bother at this late stage. She did, however, rip open an alcohol pad to drag it over her sharp little scissors, which were all she had in the kit to cut the umbilical cord with.

"Madre de dios," she heard one of the men breathe outside the windows.

Ignoring them all, Angeline kept encouraging Soledad not to push just quite yet. "Pant, one, two, three, that's right. Good, good." She grabbed a paper-wrapped spool of sterile gauze from the kit, as well as the small blue aspirator bulb, and dropped both on the crumpled dress covering Soledad's belly. "Okay, now, push. That's it. *Push,* Soledad." The baby's head emerged and Angeline caught her breath at the awesomeness of the moment.

No matter how many babies she'd helped delivered it always seemed a miracle to her.

"Keep panting, Soledad. Hold off on pushing for just a moment." She grabbed the bulb and gently, quickly suctioned the infant's nose and mouth. "All right, now. Let's finish the job now. Come on, you can do it. Push!"

The woman gave a mighty yell, hunching forward, and the rest of the baby seemed to nearly squirt right into Angeline's hands.

Soledad's head fell back against the door behind her, exhausted. Angeline joggled the slippery infant in her hands, clearing the mucus again. Already the tiny girl's skin was pinkening and she let out a mewling, very healthy howl.

Soledad cried, pressing her hands against her chest.

"Congratulations, Mama. You have a beautiful daughter," Angeline told the woman, and wrapped the baby in the blue towel that had so recently, she realized surreally, hidden a Glock in her lap. She settled the baby on the woman's belly and ripped open the gauze, cutting off a length to tie around the umbilical cord.

Behind her, the door to the car suddenly sprang open and the men began yelling again as if they'd never stopped. If it weren't for the hands Brody held out for her, Angeline would have tumbled out onto her backside.

"Easy does it," he said, holding her in place. His chin hooked over her shoulder, his chest pressed against her back. "Amazing," he murmured, looking at the tiny baby swathed in terry cloth.

Angeline finished making the knot. She could see the ambulance that had finally pulled up, so she didn't bother tying off the cord a second time in order to cut it. She'd leave that, as well as the afterbirth and washing up the baby to the emergency crew.

As it was, Angeline's wonderfully clean clothing that she'd donned after her shower were—once again—somewhat less than pristine.

With her adrenaline finally slowing,

Angeline leaned closer to the baby again. "God speed to you both," she told Soledad.

"*Gracias,* Angeline." The new mother caught Angeline's hand with her own. "*Gracias.*"

"We'd better move out of the way," Brody told her softly. The ambulance crew had wheeled a stretcher alongside the wreck.

She ducked her head inside the car just long enough to retrieve her kit, and then they were heading toward the taxi.

It was Soledad's husband who provided the distraction they needed. When he spotted the officer, he ran forward, his hands gesturing wildly as he continued sharing the tale that, Angeline suspected, would just grow in scope with each telling.

They climbed into the cab and showing great decorum, Brody backed up and turned around, pulling into the first side street he came to. Only then did he allow himself to put on some speed.

"Was it gross?" Davey was bouncing in the backseat where there was a lamentable lack of seat belts. "You sure *look* kinda gross, Angeline."

Angeline laughed a little, though her

nerves were beginning to set in, making her feel shaky.

"I don't think she looks gross at all," Brody countered.

She gave him a surprised look only to have her gaze captured for a long moment by his.

"In fact, I think she looks pretty amazing."

She swallowed. Hard.

Then he turned that disturbing intensity back onto the road in front of him and it was as if that tight, breathless connection had never occurred. "But you should ditch the T-shirt right now for something less noticeable." His voice was brusque. "God only knows whose attention we've earned *now*."

Chapter Nine

Whether or not their detour drew attention, Brody managed to drive through the city without further delay or mishap. Angeline, calling on every pragmatic cell she possessed, exchanged her soiled top right there in the front seat next to Brody for a fresh T-shirt that Eva pulled out of the duffel for her. And the shirt was left, crumpled on the floorboard right along with the taxi that he parked in a teeming lot near the airport. The lot was already congested with cars—what was one more, even if it was big, bright and yellow?

Before they caught one of the city buses that carried them to yet another corner of Caracas, Brody instructed the kids to address him and Angeline as Mom and Dad from here on out. It seemed to bother them much less than it did Angeline, who sat there twisting the mock wedding ring around and around her finger.

Once more, they were showing more resilience than she felt. And if they were feeling paralyzed with worry over their *real* parents, they weren't showing it.

The first bus was followed by three others until finally, they walked into a small, dusty building that sat at the end of an airstrip.

The International Airport it most certainly was *not.*

Fortunately, Angeline had had her share of experiences with small planes back in Wyoming, so she wasn't completely thrown when in short order they were taking off in a minuscule six-seater piloted by a smiling young man who talked a mile a minute.

He didn't seem to notice or care that Brody's responses to his nonstop dialogue were few and far between. Calling them curt would have been charitable.

As for Angeline, she was kept plenty busy keeping Davey from squirming out of his safety belt because he was insatiably curious about everything. Keeping Davey contained was better than looking out the window, though, at the expanse of water beneath them.

When they landed, without incident, in Puerto Rico, Angeline had a strong, *strong* desire to drop to her knees and kiss the dusty unpaved runway on which they'd landed. Instead, she kept the children's attention diverted from the exchange of money between Brody and the pilot.

Then it was a hair-raising cab ride—this time with the proper driver—and more money exchanged hands before they landed on the doorstep of Hacienda Paradise.

It was considerably smaller than even the hotel in Caracas had been, yet *this* one looked as if it had been designed as a vacation home away from home.

Pristine stucco looked particularly white with the vivid ochre arches over the doors and windows and the wealth of flowering bushes planted against the walls. Situated on a hillside, she could see the ocean beyond and despite the pervasively gray, cloudy sky, it was still a beautiful sight.

They went in through the colorful main door where the interior was as lovely and welcoming as the exterior. There was an expanse of gleaming terra-cotta tile, dozens of potted plants and warm rattan furnishings—all covered with cushions in varying patterns and colors that combined as a whole in pleasing results.

"Wait here," Brody said, gesturing at the collection of tropical-print-upholstered sofas in the lobby. "I haven't seen Roger in a long time and let's just say that we didn't part on the best of terms."

Angeline was too tired to let that little revelation rock her, and she was happy enough to sit and wait for whatever reception they received. The truth was, the run of sleepless nights was beginning to catch up with her. And the rattan sofas were *so* comfortable. She let out a long, soft sigh.

Beside her, Eva made a similar sound. Davey, however, was beyond overtired. He was in constant motion.

Brody crossed the tile heading toward the shining wood reception desk, but before he made it halfway, an exceedingly handsome black man, dressed completely in white, headed for him, a smile wreathing his face.

"Simon," he greeted, his English tinged with an islander's lilt. Without a moment's hesitation, he grabbed Brody in a massive bear hug, slapping him on the back.

Angeline tucked her tongue in the roof of her mouth.

Looked to her like the men were on pretty good terms.

And obviously, she'd been right about "Simon" being another one of Brody's aliases. She watched him turn toward her, extending his long arm. "Darling," he called, using the most perfect British accent she'd ever heard, "come and meet my old friend, Roger."

"Why'd he call him *Simon*," Davey whispered.

Angeline gave Eva a look as she slowly rose.

"That's his name for now," Eva whispered to her brother, pulling him onto her lap. "Don't forget."

"But I thought we was supposed to call him Mr. Dad."

"Just Dad. We are. Shh. We don't want anyone to hear."

Angeline gave them an encouraging smile and continued forward. Her conscience niggled at her for approving of the quick way they adapted to deception. It was disquieting how easily she stomped out that niggling, too.

She reached Brody and Roger and pinned what she hoped was a natural-looking smile on her face. Keeping it firmly in place when Brody slung his arm around her shoulders and pulled her up snug against his side took even more effort.

"Roger Sterling, this is my beautiful wife, Angie. Darling, this old reprobate is an old...friend of mine."

Roger clasped her hand in both of his, bending low to kiss the back of it. "Beautiful Angie. Welcome to my Hacienda. But what your Simon isn't telling you is that we used to work together."

Brody squeezed her shoulder when she gave a little start. "Oh?" She managed to look enquiringly up at her "husband."

"That was aeons ago, Rog." Brody smiled at her. "Back in our ideological youth."

"Youth?" Roger tossed back his head and laughed. "Not even those ten—no, it's twelve years ago now—could you or I claim youthfulness. Now, who are those young ones over there watching us with big brown eyes? Surely not—"

"Angie's kids," Simon-Brody said. "I'm afraid her first husband—"

"—don't bore the man with that old tale, darling," Angeline interrupted. She looked up at Roger who was nearly as tall as Brody. "Simon's a wonderful father," she lied as if she'd been doing it all her life. And it wasn't all a lie, because the fact was, Brody was good with the children. "He even insists on bringing them with us every time we go on vacation."

"So this *is* a holiday?" Roger looked back at Simon. "I'm wounded, old man. You should have given me some notice. As it is, I have only two rooms available."

"We're actually on our way back to the States. If you can let us hole up for one night, we'll be—"

"Sure, sure." Roger lifted his hand, cutting off Simon's words as he went back to the reception desk. He produced an old-fashioned key and came back, dropping it into Brody's palm. "Nothing but the best for my old debating partner. Do you have luggage?"

"Nothing we can't manage," Simon-Brody

assured. He looked at the room key, on which Angeline could see engraved in gold the number ten. "This have a good location?"

"The best," Roger assured. "Perfect view of the pool in one direction and the ocean in the other. I'll have one of my boys show you back."

"No need." Brody slid his hand down Angeline's arm, linking his fingers through hers. "We'll catch up later, after we've had a chance to settle the kids."

Roger's smile was still in place as Brody collected the children in their wake and they all headed back out the front door and around to the side where he'd left her duffel and the children's purloined pillowcase.

"So, *Simon,* you worked with him, did you?"

He ignored her soft comment, and continued striding along the flower-lined sidewalk until they reached the end of the lovely building.

The door Brody stopped at was in the very rear of the courtyard. He unlocked it, quickly set their ragtag belongings inside, and then ushered them in. He pressed his fingers to his lips as he shut the door and fastened the locks.

All four of them.

She frowned a little at the sight of so many

locks, and then leaned back against the door
as he went into the same hunt-and-seek mode
that he'd used at the convent.

Since this room was not a room at all, but
a suite, she expected that it might take him
some time to appease his paranoia.

Eva pointed to the couch, silently checking
with Brody before throwing herself down on
it when he nodded. Brody had already turned
on the television, and she picked up the
remote, slowly flipping through the channels
that offered a seemingly dizzying assortment
of options.

Angeline unlatched Davey from her hip
and picked him up. His head snuggled down
into the crook of her neck. "Come on, bud,"
she whispered. "Let's you and I go have a lie
down." She peeked through the open
doorways. The first was a bathroom—
standard, albeit well-appointed.

She passed it by for the next doorway. A
bedroom. Two twin beds, each with its own
chair, table and lamp beside it. The last
doorway, separated from the other two by a
neatly appointed kitchenette, contained only
one bed, which looked wide enough to sail
home on. Attached to that was another

bathroom, this time with a tub large enough for a party.

At least a party of two.

The guilty thought taunted her as she turned tail and headed back to the twin beds.

There, she curled up on the wonderfully soft mattress with Davey tucked against her. She felt reasonably confident that if she kept him still for even five minutes, he'd get the nap he badly needed.

Sleep dragged enticingly at her, and she told herself she'd just grab a nap. A little one.

Then she could face whatever was next on Brody's plan.

While Angeline napped, Brody finished searching every inch of the bedroom right around them.

He added the surveillance bugs he found there to the small pile of them that was growing on the top of the fancy, satellite-fed television.

On the couch, Eva was sleeping, too. She'd lasted all of ten minutes after Angeline and Davey had hit the mattress.

Catching some shut-eye himself was mighty appealing, but first he'd finish searching out the rest of the suite.

One advantage was that Roger hadn't changed his style over the past decade. When Brody felt reasonably confident that he'd discovered every listening device, he dropped them by handfuls into a glass pitcher that he found conveniently provided in the nicely equipped kitchenette.

Then he filled the pitcher with water and stuck the entire thing inside the refrigerator.

Roger would be pissed, but Brody didn't care.

Then, he went into the main bedroom with its decadent bathroom en suite. He tossed Angeline's duffel on the dresser and rooted shamelessly through it until he found her first-aid kit. He flipped it open, cataloging the contents, and then worked the T-shirt over his head, managing not to dislodge the bandage that he'd taped there what seemed days earlier.

It hadn't been days, though.

It had just been that morning, before dawn.

"Oh, my *God*."

He whipped his head around, wincing as the adhesive tape he'd slapped copiously around the mound of gauze pads over his ribcage pulled. "I thought you were sleeping," he groused.

Angeline's lips were parted, her gaze trained on the less-than-professional work he'd made of the bandage. She stopped next to him and prodded her fingers none too gently against his shoulder. "Turn so I can see better. Good Lord, Br—Simon, who taped up this mess?"

"*I* did," he admitted grumpily. He didn't assure her that the suite was safe to speak openly, though.

She huffed, and began picking at the edge of one long strip. "It clearly didn't occur to you to say something about this earlier." Her voice was snippy, a perfect accompaniment to her withering expression. She freed the edge finally and took definite delight in yanking it off his skin.

He winced. "Hells bells, woman. Go a little easy there."

She tore another strip, literally, off his hide. "Why? You're the big macho man who doesn't have to admit to any sort of weakness." She yanked a third off.

He yelped and covered her hand with his. "Dammit! What is this? Nurse Ratchet has replaced the saintly Florence?"

But he realized that her hand beneath his was trembling.

"Dammit," he said again, only this time with far less heat.

He slid his arm around her shoulders as she turned into him, burying her face against his chest, inches above where the gauze had done a reasonable job of keeping the seeping knife wound from staining his shirt.

Her hand swept up his spine. "What happened?" Her voice was muffled, her words warm puffs against his flesh. "*Was* it our, uh, our friend? No wonder you were so furious when I insisted on stopping to help Soledad."

"It wasn't him." He circled her braid with his fingers; it was thick as her wrist and silkier than anything he'd ever felt in his life. So much for thinking that he'd keep her at a distance if she thought they might be listened in on. "Merely a couple blokes who didn't appreciate me interrupting their drug deal."

"Merely." She shuddered against him. "God. You should have said something sooner. Like when you came back to the hotel this morning."

"We were already running late. Too late."

She tilted back her head, her dark eyebrows pulling together. Her hand settled over his bandaging as gently as a whisper.

In its way, that soft touch was more painful than her wrenching off the sticking adhesive strips.

"This is why you weren't back before dawn."

"Yes."

She moistened her lips and ducked her forehead against his chest again. Ground it softly against him.

A whole new set of pain surged; the kind he couldn't—wouldn't—allay.

As if realizing it, she went still for a gut-twisting moment. Then she took a step back. The thick ridges of her braid slid smoothly out of his hand.

She gathered up the first-aid kit. "Come into the bathroom," she said. "There's probably better light in there." She led the way, turning on every light—and there were a good half-dozen of them.

"Sit there." She gestured at the wide plank of earth-toned granite that spanned the distance between the two hammered copper sinks.

He sat.

She ran water until it was hot in one of the sinks, and wet one of the thick washcloths, which she then held over the adhesive, helping to loosen what he now considered an overly effective death grip. Then patiently, she managed to coax the strips loose until she could peel away the gauze that he'd bunched together over the slash.

She sucked in a hard breath when she saw the extent of the wound. She tossed the gauze into the other unused sink. "This should have been sutured."

"I didn't have a lot of free time," he reminded, trying not to wince like a damn baby.

But, *Christ,* it hurt.

Her slender, deft fingers moving on him were causing plenty of their own torment, too.

She made a soft hmming sound, and wet another cloth with warm water, which she used to clean away the dried blood around the perimeter of the gash. "How, exactly, did this happen? There were two of them?"

"Three."

She hmmed again. It reminded him of his mother, actually, whenever she was withholding judgment over his defense of some mischief he and Penny had gotten into.

For once, thinking of his sister didn't make everything inside him want to shut down. Maybe it was just because it seemed to be happening more often, lately.

Maybe it was just the company he was keeping of late.

She cast a look up at him through her lashes. The compress carefully moved over the gash and drizzled warm water over it. "And?"

She was using plenty of water. It slid down his belly, soaking into his jeans. At the rate she was going, he'd be out of dry pants for the rest of the day.

"And nothing. They didn't like me interrupting them."

"But where were you? Where'd this happen? At the All-Med office, or after?"

"After."

She pursed her lips, bringing into evidence that little dimple below her lips—situated there like some pretty birthmark on a long-ago pinup girl. "I don't suppose you went to the police."

"No." His voice was dry.

"How'd you get the supplies to bandage yourself up?"

"You mean the stellar example of proper first aid that you so admire?"

The dimple disappeared as she smiled. "Ah, now there's the wit I know." She dropped the sopping cloth back into the water in the sink, sending a small cascade over the edge where it soaked into his jeans.

"I'm going to need to use Roger's damn laundry service," he muttered.

"Where *did* you get the clothes?"

"In the same drugstore where I pinched the gauze and tape."

"You actually found a drugstore that was open at that hour?"

He gave her a look.

"Oh, dear." She sighed faintly. "Does it not bother you *at all* to avail yourself of… of…things that don't belong to you?"

"Nobody's going out of business as a result of it," he defended drily. "And the trucks have all gone back to their rightful owners, assuming that your peeps at All-Med made it up to St. Agnes already." When things got back to normal, he might just have to satisfy his curiosity over who'd donated that unusual equipment to the convent…and why.

"There's the Jeep we left stuck in the mud."

"Hey. I'll have you know that I purchased that decrepit transport, and paid a few bucks *more* than I ought to have, considering its deplorable condition."

"Really." She stepped back, holding the

tube of antiseptic aloft. "Who'd you buy it from then?"

"Some lad in Puerto Grande, if you must know." If he'd heard that defensive tone in anyone else's voice he'd have laughed up-roariously. As it was, he was considerably annoyed by it. "His whole family was trying to sell off nearly all their belongings," he finished. "A bicycle missing a wheel, a radio that was a good twenty years old, a sway-backed excuse of a mule. They were trying to get enough together to pay for the kid's sister's first—"

"—first semester of college," she finished, taking the words right out of his mouth.

He frowned. "Yeah."

"Puerto Grande is a small village," she murmured. "We all knew about the Zamora family. Brisa is the youngest and will be the first member of their family ever to go to college. *You're* the one who bought their Jeep."

"Isn't that what I've been trying to say?"

She smiled softly and stepped forward again, right into the vee of his legs. Her chocolate-brown eyes were on a level with his mouth, and their focus seemed to be fixated there. "What am I going to do about you, Mr. Simon?"

He dug his fingers into the granite on either side of him.

Of course, the stone didn't have a helluva lot of give.

Not like the gilded skin stretched taut over her supple arms would.

He deliberately racked his head against the expanse of mirror behind him.

"You're going to bandage me up," he said, but his voice was gruff. Damn near hoarse.

"In a minute," she whispered. She leaned into him, tilting her head, and light as a whisper, she rubbed her lips over his.

Chapter Ten

She'd started out feeling tenderness.

That was all, Angeline assured herself. Just tenderness for this man whose unexpected acts of kindness touched her just as much as his more "creative" stunts shocked her.

But tenderness was abruptly eaten up in the incendiary flames that rose far too rapidly for her to fight.

Instead, she stood there, caught, as a wildfire seemed to lick through both of them.

His arm came around her shoulders, an iron band holding her needlessly in place, his mouth as hungry as hers. A sound, raw and full of want, rose in her throat—or was it his?

She couldn't tell, and didn't much care, as he pulled her tighter against him, tighter until she felt the heat of his bare chest burning through her T-shirt, tighter until she felt that undeniably hard ridge rising and pushing against her, making her want to writhe against him in response.

Her fingers pressed greedily into the sinewy muscles cording his bare shoulders and she dragged in a hoarse breath when his lips burned from hers, down over her cheek. Her jaw. Her neck.

His hand curled around her braid, tugging her head back more, until he touched his tongue to the pulse beating frantically at the base of her throat. Again that needful moan filled the room.

It was definitely coming from her. A thoroughly unfamiliar sound—one that was vaguely shocking in some far distant reach of her mind.

She stared up blindly at the gleaming light fixture above their heads. Pinpoints of light shone in her mind, less from the bulbs than from the dazzling wonder of his touch.

Without conscious direction, her hands

slid over those wide, wide shoulders, around his neck, into his brown hair that slipped, smooth and thick, through her sifting fingers.

Her braid bunched in his hand, he cupped the back of her head, pulling her mouth back to his. His other hand swept down her spine, around her hip, between them, urging her closer, closer—

"Ouch, oh, sh—" He yanked his head back, knocking his head against the mirror again, this time far less intentionally. "*Bloody* hell."

Angeline froze, reason returning with one swift, hard kick.

She stared at his chest, at the hideous knife wound running parallel to his ribs that looked as if it would bleed again at any moment, at his large hand still cupped over her breast.

His thumb moved, rubbing over the tight hard crest that only rose even more greedily for him.

Horrified at herself, she jerked back, snatching up the antiseptic tube from the floor that she'd dropped somewhere along the way.

Like when she'd been dragging her hands all over his body, completely forgetting the basic fact that the poor man was wounded!

"I'm sorry," she said quickly. She fumbled with the threaded top on the tube. She got it off, only to have the tiny top slip through her shaking fingers. "I...I don't know what I was thinking."

"I know what *I* was thinking." His voice was even deeper than usual. Huskier.

And it sent another ribbon of desire bolting through the ribbon parade already working from her heart down to knees that felt as substantial as jelly.

"I shouldn't have done that." She licked her lips, forcing her attention to stay on his wound as she squeezed an uneven glob of antibiotic cream over it.

He sucked in a hard breath, the ridged muscles of his abdomen jerking. "No, *that* you shouldn't have done," he muttered, and caught the hand delivering the cream and dragged it away before she could do more damage.

She sank her teeth into her tongue for a long moment, trying to master the burning behind her eyes before she did something even more embarrassing than throwing herself at him. "I need to d-dress your wound."

His teeth bared slightly. His eyes were slits of blue between his narrowed lashes.

"Pardon me if I tell you that I'd rather *you* just simply undress."

Angeline felt as if she'd lost her ability to speak.

So she just stood there.

Staring at him.

Wanting him.

He looked like an oversized jungle cat, lying in wait for his prey to draw near. And *she* was the prey.

"Here."

She blinked, looking stupidly at the packet of gauze pads he'd picked up from the kit beside him.

"Come on, Angie. Finish the job."

Angie. And spoken in that perfectly British accent that she realized, belatedly, he hadn't dropped for even one moment.

She sucked in another hard breath, this one formed of cold, hard mortification.

He suspected they were being listened in on. He'd done his usual search and destroy, but had he found some sort of bug, after all?

Had someone really been *listening* to them?

To her? To that utterly sexual moan that had flowed out of her, more than once?

She racked her brains, trying to think if

she'd said his name, as well—God, it had been screaming through her mind, her body—

She snatched the packet from him and tore it open. Tossed the sterile packaging aside to gently fit the gauze over his wound. "It would be better if I had a few butterflies instead of just this gauze to pull it together more tightly." The hoarseness of her voice went a long way toward diffusing her brusque words.

"Keep talking, babe." He'd tilted his head back slightly, watching her from beneath his lashes. "I'm getting hotter by the second."

She flushed and layered on more gauze, creating a cushioned dressing. He pulled the spool of tape from the kit and held it looped over his finger.

Unfortunately, his finger was attached to his hand that was resting on the very firm bulge of thigh covered in somewhat damp denim.

She swallowed on her dry throat again, and slid the tape off his finger, trying to pretend that she wasn't perfectly aware of his erection mere inches away.

She tore off a length of tape and carefully sealed the edges of the dressing. "This is paper tape. It won't hurt when we have to change it," she assured, putting all of her effort into keeping her voice steady and smooth, and failing miserably. "But you'll want to keep it dry, so when you shower, we'll cover it with plastic first."

"Easier to take a bath. You can wash my back."

Her gaze slid guiltily to the enormous built-for-two tub and she knew, if he told her to turn on the taps right that instant, she'd have been hard pressed not to do just that. No matter that the walls might have ears, no matter that Eva was sound asleep in one room on the couch and Davey in another.

No matter that she'd never shared a bath with any man, much less shared her body.

When it came to Brody-Hewitt-Simon Paine, she feared she was excruciatingly willing to share *everything*.

She pressed her palms together, feeling the wedding ring on her finger. It no longer felt so strange wearing the gold band.

Which was a realization that on its own was enough to make her feel somewhat daunted.

"Do, uh, do you need something for the pain? I've only got over-the-counter stuff, I'm afraid, but you could take a prescription dosage of it."

"Is that the only pain you're willing to take care of?"

She opened her mouth. Closed it again before the assurance came out that she didn't really mean, anyway. Instead, she admitted the raw truth. "No."

His eyes narrowed again. He let out a hiss between his teeth. "You know how to make it hard on a man, don't you." His voice seemed to come up from somewhere deep inside him.

She flushed all over again.

"No pun intended," he added.

The flush grew even hotter.

He sat forward, wincing a little as he pressed his palm against the new dressing, and straightened from the granite countertop. "You know, it's a lot easier to resist you when I think you're going to be strong enough for the both of us. If you're going to look at me with those eyes a man could drown in and be *honest* like that, I don't know what the hell to do with you."

Her eyebrows rose with sudden boldness. "You don't *know?*"

He gave a short laugh. "Angeli—" He bit off the rest of her name.

She pressed her lips together.

"I don't often forget myself," he murmured. He lifted his hand and brushed the back of his finger down her cheek. "But you sure do have a way of getting me right to that point."

Her knees evidently decided jelly was too substantial, and dissolved into water instead.

Then he closed his hand around hers and drew her out of the sinful bathroom, past the bed she couldn't bring herself to look at and back into the main room where he opened the door of the refrigerator and gestured.

Angeline peered at the pitcher of water, which was the only thing inside, except for the gleaming shelves. "Good grief. Are those—?" At least three inches of metallic-looking discs—each no larger than a watch battery—were sunk in the water, filling the bottom of the pitcher.

Brody nodded.

He'd told her that paranoia kept him sane, but she'd sort of taken that as an exaggeration.

Looking at those dozens of discs now, she wasn't so sure it was an exaggeration.

Not when they were dauntingly real.

He pushed the refrigerator door closed again.

Angeline folded her arms tightly over her chest and looked around, as if she'd be able to see if there were any more bugs still hidden around. That, of course, was as likely as her being able to jump over the moon.

If Brody hadn't found them, why on earth would she?

"You think there might be others?" She looked back at him, only to find his gaze fixed on her arms, folded across her breasts.

The ribbon parade inside her jumped right back into action, sliding into an all-out rumba.

"Possibly."

She dropped her arms and deliberately turned her back on him, looking over at Eva, who still slept, sprawled facedown on the sofa. The television remote control sat on the rattan table next to the sofa. The device wouldn't be very useful, unless Brody saw fit to put the parts back together.

"Is this how Roger always greets you? With such, well, such *nice* accommodations?"

"Pretty much."

"But he said you worked together. With—" She didn't know what she could dare to say—whether she ought not to mention

Hollins-Winword—but Brody, showing his usual perception, understood, anyway.

He shook his head.

Roger had talked about their association being twelve years past. But Angeline had been quite sure Brody had been with Hollins-Winword since his very early twenties. He'd told her that the very first time they'd met. She'd told him about coming from Wyoming and he'd told her he didn't come from anywhere.

And then he'd given her a gargantuan flirtatious grin and told her that if she needed anyone to show her the ropes, he had plenty that he'd be willing to lasso around her.

"Then what did you and he…" She trailed off when he lifted his hand. The universal *stop* sign.

She sighed. Her curiosity would have to go unappeased, obviously. At least for now. But later, she fully intended to discover more about the things that made Brody tick.

"I'm going to go out and stretch my legs," he said abruptly. "You'll be fine here, though. If you need anything, just ring Roger."

She looked toward the door again, with its four substantial locks. Not even in her apartment in Atlanta did she have that much security on her door. "Are you, uh, going to take the girl?"

He smiled suddenly. "Delilah, you mean? Yes."

Obviously, he didn't worry about someone wondering who Delilah was. "Are you going to try to reach your—" handler "—friend about our travel arrangements?"

"That's the plan."

"Will you be gone long?"

"Why? You going to miss me?" He tilted his head closer to hers, his voice dropping even lower. "Go swim in that big tub while I'm gone," he suggested. "Think of me."

She pursed her lips together, giving him an annoyed look that didn't fool him for a solitary second, if the unholy gleam in his eyes was anything to go by.

He disappeared into the bedroom and came out a minute later, the blue T-shirt back in place. He hadn't tucked it in, though, and she assumed that was all the better to hide Delilah with.

"The children will need to eat when they wake," she told him, wondering if whoever was listening—*if* anyone was listening— thought she sounded like a proper wife.

"Then eat," he said simply.

Which made her feel idiotic. As if he thought she couldn't make a simple decision like that. "I *meant,* would you prefer that we wait for you to return, so we can all eat together." That's what families did mostly. At least in her experience.

Her parents had sat down at the dinner table nearly every night with her and J.D. and Casey while they'd been growing up. They'd talk about their day, sometimes they'd argue, but far more often than that, there was laughter.

And always there had been the security of knowing their roots were set in an unshakeable foundation.

It was the kind of home she'd wanted to make someday for *her* children, if she ever had any. These days, that desire had come less and less frequently, though. Not because she still didn't want it someday, but because it had become more difficult to see herself sitting across her own dinner table from the man of her dreams.

"Touching," he said, which made her search his expression for amusement.

But she found none and realized that was even more disturbing.

"I'll probably be back in an hour or so. If I'm not, go on down to the restaurant. Have Roger charge it to the room." At *that*, he did look amused.

Which made her wonder if he intended to finagle his way out of paying for their lodgings altogether. She'd have asked, but assumed that was probably not one of those things he'd want to be possibly overheard.

"And if you're longer than that?" She couldn't help but think about his cautions back in Caracas.

She didn't need to elaborate. He understood, perfectly. "Same thing I said before still stands."

They were staying in a room that had been bugged, presumably by the owner himself. Yet he nevertheless believed the man would get her and the children back to the States, just because "Simon" had asked him to.

"I think there's an interesting story in there somewhere," she murmured.

"Not one worth the effort of retelling." He headed for the door, stopped short and backtracked, surprising her right out of her sanity again when he pressed a hard, fast kiss to her mouth.

She swayed unsteadily when he straightened and stepped away from her. His sharp eyes, of course, noticed her swaying around like a tree in a hurricane, and he gave a little nod. "Good," he murmured. "Glad I'm not the only one thrown for a loop." Then he strode to the door, flipped open the multiple locks and peered out.

Evidently, *some* things didn't change, just because they were currently ensconced in considerably nicer—albeit possibly surveilled—digs. "Lock these after me."

She was already heading for the door to do so.

A moment later, he was gone.

She slid the substantial locks into place and turned back to face the lovely suite. She suddenly felt cold, and it wasn't only the reminder that their purpose there at all wasn't a lighthearted one.

Hewitt and Sophia Stanley were still out there somewhere, being held against their will, and their children *were* in danger, as well.

What also had Angeline shivering, though, was the realization that for the first time in her life, she could put a face on the man who sat on the other side of the dinner table from her, with their children scattered along in between in that lovely image of the future.

Brody's face.

Yet he was the man who had—within the last forty-eight hours, no less—admitted that he had no yearning desire to stay in any one place for any particular length of time.

He was the least likely person she knew who'd ever even want that dinnertime ritual with the family, who'd want to see the sun rise and set day after day over the same horizon, much less the same home.

So what was she doing?

Was she keeping the man at arm's length, never taking his flirtations seriously, never letting herself get swept into the wake of his appeal?

No.

She was throwing herself right into his arms, and no amount of reminding herself all the reasons why doing so again would be a monumental mistake seemed to be enough to keep her from taking that flight again. Because, right or wrong, Angeline finally faced the truth.

She was in love with Brody Paine.

Chapter Eleven

Considerably more than an "hour or two" had passed before Brody returned later that day.

As Angeline had predicted, the kids had been ravenous when they'd awakened. Very aware of the bugs that Brody might not have discovered, she decided it was better to take Eva and Davey down to the restaurant.

She'd been afraid that the kids might slip—call her by her name or something, but they never did. Not even when Roger, insisting on meeting their every culinary desire— right up to and including Davey's requested deep-fried macaroni and cheese—had sat down at the table with them had they given anything away.

If anything, she was as wary of something coming out of *her* mouth. Squelching her curiosity over just how Brody and Roger were connected was nigh impossible, though she managed.

Just.

While Roger, on the other hand, seemed to feel free in asking plenty of his own questions about her relationship with Simon.

She tap danced her way around giving the man direct answers as much as she could, but feared she wasn't really fooling anyone.

Then, when Roger had turned his focus on the children, and asked how they thought their stepfather rated, she sat forward, giving Eva and Davey steady looks in return to the startled ones they gave her.

"They think he's wonderful, obviously," she assured Roger on their behalf. "Of course they love their father, as they should. But Simon has been good to all of us." She turned and smiled, full wattage, into his face, knowing perfectly well the effect that usually had on most members of the male species.

"And what about you, Roger? Any woman and child keeping your home fire burning?"

His speculative smile turned regretful. "If there were a beautiful woman such as you who wished to burn any fires with me, I'd certainly consider setting several."

"Stop flattering my wife, old man," Brody said, appearing almost out of nowhere beside their table. He slid his hand, deliberately proprietary, over Angeline's shoulder, and left it there. "Just because you haven't found a woman of your own is no reason to go poaching in my territory."

"What is this accusation of flattery about?" Roger pressed his hand across his heart. "I speak only the truth."

Angeline just laughed lightly, and pushed her chair back, rising from the table. "My head spins," she assured. "But you'll have to excuse us. The children get restless if they sit too long at the dinner table." It was a blatant exaggeration and one that she felt slightly guilty for offering.

But only slightly.

Eva, Angeline noticed as the girl tucked her napkin under the edge of her half-empty plate, was looking a little flushed again. "The meal was very good," she said politely. "Thank you." She elbowed Davey.

"Thank you," he echoed, rubbing his side and giving her an aggrieved look.

"I'll join you in a few, love," Simon-Brody told her. "Roger and I have some catching up to do."

"Of course." She sent a smile Roger's way again, and ushered the children away from the table. She couldn't help wondering if the "catching up" had to do with the matter of getting the four of them back to the States.

"Can we swim?" Davey asked as they left the restaurant. They could see the pool through the gleaming windows overlooking the courtyard area of the hotel.

Angeline resisted the urge to look back at Brody. "Do you know how to swim?"

"My dad taught us," Davey said.

"We're s'posed to wait an hour after eating before swimming," Eva said, giving him a severe look.

"I think that's an old wives' tale," Angeline murmured.

"And besides, we don't have our swim-suits with us," the girl reminded.

They left the lobby behind and headed across

the courtyard. "You've got a T-shirt and shorts," Angeline said. "You could wear that. In fact, let's just stop at the swimming pool, right now. You can roll up your jeans and dangle your legs over the side, at the very least."

"Yippee." Davey grabbed Angeline around the thighs and hugged her. He darted toward the pool.

Muffling an oath, Angeline nudged Eva ahead of her, hurrying after his precipitous race for the pool. In contrast to Davey's energy, Eva, however, was showing very little.

Angeline slipped her hand along Eva's ponytail. "Everything is going to be all right," she told her softly.

"I'm not a baby. You don't have to say things that might not be true." Eva sounded fierce, but Angeline still recognized the need beneath that begged for reassurance.

Her heart squeezed. She stopped there in the middle of the narrow sidewalk, facing Eva. Amidst the profusion of lovely flowering shrubs, it seemed hard to believe that anything terrible could touch them.

But Angeline had seen too much in her work to let herself believe that "prettiness" provided any sort of substantial barrier against disaster.

"I don't think you're a baby, Eva," she said with perfect truthfulness. "And I'm not lying because I think you can't handle the truth. I truly believe that this all will turn out fine in the end."

"Because of, um, Simon."

Angeline smiled faintly. She smoothed her hand along Eva's ponytail again. "Between him and the three of us, I think we've made a pretty good team." She slipped her hand beneath Eva's small, pointed chin. "Keep your faith strong, sweetheart. Amazing things can result."

Her eyes shimmered. "My mom says stuff like that," she whispered.

Angeline let out a long sigh, and leaned down, hugging the girl's narrow shoulders. She knew she'd made the right move when Eva hugged her back. Tightly.

Her throat closed a little. What brave children the Stanleys were. "And I can't wait to meet her and tell both her and your dad what a fabulous pair of kids they've got," she said just as softly.

"I just wish I could talk to them." Eva's fists pounded against Angeline's shoulders in frustration.

"I know, honey. I know."

* * *

From his vantage point in Roger's second-floor office, Brody had a clear view of the courtyard and the pool. He saw Davey yanking off his tennis shoes and rolling up his pants. Saw Angeline stop and talk with solemn-faced Eva, then after a while, not looking quite so serious, they joined Davey poolside.

Soon all three of them were sitting on the edge of the pool, their pants up around their knees, as they kicked and splashed each other.

"You haven't told her, have you." Roger sat at his desk, where he'd just finished making the arrangements to help get them out of the country.

Brody leaned his shoulder against the tall window, taking his gaze off Angeline and the kids only long enough to scan the courtyard. Seeing nothing unusual among the lush landscape, he looked back at his *family.* "No point."

"You and I go back a long way, Simon."

"Too long," Brody drawled.

"We would have made a great team," Roger continued, ignoring the interruption. "If you hadn't bailed on me."

"I didn't bail."

"We didn't exactly hang out our shingle,

either, my friend." Roger's voice never lost the gait of his native Jamaica, but now it sounded pretty dry. "Sterling and Brody," he reminded. "Attorneys at Law."

"Brody and Sterling," he corrected blandly. "And just because I didn't keep with the plan didn't mean *you* had to ditch it for all this." He gestured out the window. "You were never with Hollins as long as I was, anyway."

"True." Brody heard, rather than saw the fatalistic shrug his one-time partner gave. "I was recruited out of university, while you—"

"I was recruited out of grade school," Brody muttered, exaggerating only slightly. He'd been fifteen when his family was killed, and fifteen when he'd been taken under the wing of Hollins-Winword's main man, the infamous Coleman Black.

Warm and fuzzy, though, it had not been.

"I never did understand why you stay with the agency when you hate them as much as you do."

"The agency makes freaks out of us all," Brody murmured. Not even Roger knew just how "close" a relationship Brody'd had with Cole. "That's not hate. That's plain fact. Look at the way you decorate your suites around this place." He shot Roger a dry look.

"You don't have to worry about your privacy," Roger added, drolly. "I only monitor the room when I have something to gain from it."

"Sounding like your pirate roots are showing, there, Rog."

Roger's teeth flashed, but his expression stayed sober. "If you didn't like what the agency was making of us, then you shouldn't have gone back in. You left it, Simon. You were free of it all. So was I."

Yet Brody had walked away from the legal practice they'd planned. He'd had a taste of what life—normal life—could be like, and he'd bolted just when he'd been on the verge of feasting on all that normalcy. He'd gone right back to the agency that had failed in keeping his family safe.

He was well aware of the twisted reasoning and wasn't sure if it was better or worse than the other reason he'd gone back.

Because Cole had asked him to.

"You should tell her."

Trust Roger not to let an issue drop. He'd obviously never lost his liking for tenacity.

"Why didn't *you* stick with the legal career? Why go into the hotel business? *Here?*" Brody and Sterling, Attorneys at Law, was supposed to have been located in Connecticut, not coincidentally very far from the factory that fronted Hollins-Winword's center of operations.

"We all have our paths to walk, my friend. My path brought me back here."

"The woman you loved died here," Brody said. He knew that Brigitte's death during her and Roger's last year of college had been the incident that propelled him into the cold bosom of Hollins-Winword. They'd wanted to close the human trafficking ring in which Roger's girlfriend had unknowingly strayed during a spring break vacation with two of her friends.

All three young women had disappeared, their bodies never recovered.

"The last place Brigitte was seen was in the hellhole of a place right on this very location," Roger agreed evenly. "So when it came up for sale eight years ago, I tore it down and built paradise for her, instead. That's my path. Tell Angie who you are, Simon. I recognize that ring she's wearing."

He wished he'd been more sparing with the details of their situation. He'd known Roger would help, he just hadn't wanted to have to ask for it. But the situation was definitely turning for the worse. The sooner Brody got them all back in the U.S. where he could squirrel them away in a location that he *could* trust, the better.

"Every *case* matters to me," he countered flatly. "And who I *am* is Brody Paine. Simon Brody should have died a long time ago."

"Just because your family did, doesn't mean *you* should have, as well."

He didn't bother answering. The argument was old and hadn't been worth fighting even when it was new. "When's the pilot going to be ready to leave?"

"As soon as the ink is dry on the passports." Roger may have left the agency behind, but he hadn't lost some of his more creative talents. "You'll be welcomed back into the States with opened arms and nary a question," he assured. "If Santina's guy is on your trail, he's not going to follow it beyond here."

"The agency could still use you."

Roger just shook his head. "I've made my place, here. And my peace. I am content. You should try it."

"Not cut out for it, I'm afraid." Brody finally turned away from the bird's-eye-view window. "I appreciate the assistance."

"What are old partners for?"

Roger's voice rang in Brody's ears as he headed down to join Angeline by the pool. To hear Roger talk, one would think they'd been partners for decades rather than just two years.

But, he was also the only regular partner that Brody had ever been assigned.

Look how well *that* had turned out.

They'd both decided to leave the agency and open a law practice. Some stupid-ass dream of following in their fathers' footsteps.

Funny how it had turned out. Or not so funny, really, since it turned out that Brody pretty much *was* following in his father's footsteps.

Just not the man that, for the first fifteen years of his life, he'd thought had been his father.

He pushed away the memories at the same time he pushed through the glass doors and entered the courtyard. The sky was still heavy and thick with clouds, but the afternoon air felt warm and sultry.

And when Angeline lifted her head,

watching his approach with a faint smile on her face, it wasn't only the air that felt warm.

Tell her, Roger had said.

But what would be the point? He didn't talk about his past with anyone. Roger only knew part of it because Brody had clued him in one drunken night. Roger had told Brody about Brigitte's death. And Brody had told Rog about his parents, the barrister and the surgeon.

Angeline had drawn her legs out of the water, and she pushed to her bare feet, watching him with those dark, melted-chocolate eyes. "You're looking very serious," she murmured when his steps carried him to her side. "Did you reach your friend?"

Translate that to handler, he knew.

Admitting that he hadn't would only emphasize to her what a deep kettle of stinking fish they'd landed in. But he was coming to realize that voicing the lies he was used to wasn't as easy when he was looking square into her lovely oval face.

It was almost laughable, really, when Brody's entire existence for nearly as long as she'd been alive had been a string of lies, one right after another.

The only truth had been the agency—and

the man who ran it—who held in its grip the end of all of those strings. Like some damn collection of balloons.

Only if there had ever been any cheery balloons being held aloft on the end of all those strings, they'd long ago popped, leaving nothing but tatters in their place.

"No," he said, opting for truth in at least this one thing.

She drew her brows together. Her concern evident, she touched his arm, only to press her lips together and pull away again. She crossed her arms and the ring on her finger glinted softly. "You think something's gone wrong."

There were two reasons why a handler would maintain silence like this. Because their security was broken, in which case the agent was on his own, or because the agency found itself in the rare position of needing deniability. In which case, the agent was on his own.

Either way, the agent was on his own.

Even Brody wasn't protected from that protocol.

He pushed his fingers through his hair. There were a few scenarios he could think of that would prompt either option, and none of them were pretty.

"Simon?" She was still waiting.

"The last woman to call me Simon was my mother," he murmured.

Her eyes went wide. "I—" She shook her head a little, as if to dislodge whatever words were stuck in that long throat of hers that just begged for him to taste.

"Come on." Proving that he was still a coward when it came to dealing with anything really personal, he turned toward the kids who were splashing at the edge of the pool. "Move it out," he told them. "We've got a plane to catch."

He looked back at Angeline.

She was still staring at him as if she'd never seen him before. "Where are we flying to?" Her voice was faint.

"The one place that I actually trust we'll all be safe," he said quietly. "Wyoming."

Chapter Twelve

Angeline had expected that they would be flying on another small, private plane.

Brody…Simon…what*ever* his name really was, was full of his usual surprises though. After she'd gathered the children from the pool and they'd cleaned up once more, Roger had driven them to the airport himself. Before he'd dropped them off, though, he'd handed Brody a manila envelope.

The false passports that Brody produced for the four of them from that envelope didn't garner so much as a second glance from airport security. With a few minutes to spare, Simon and Angie Black, along with their two children Eva and Davey, were boarding the jet bound for home.

Roger had even managed first-class seats.

The day seemed as if it had been going on forever, but when they landed in Miami, the sun was still hanging over the horizon, though barely. Brody bought them all pizza in one of the airport food courts. His cash reserve, she suspected, had to be nearly depleted, just from the cost of getting them out of Caracas. How he'd purchased the four first-class tickets back to Florida was a mystery.

Maybe he'd borrowed from Roger.

Her curiosity had to go unanswered, however, as they barely had time to finish eating before they were boarding another flight.

This time bound for Seattle.

As a route to Wyoming, it was definitely going around the long way.

What followed was the most exhausting, circuitous route that Angeline could never have imagined even in her worst nightmares. More than thirty-six hours had passed since they'd left Miami when Brody finally, finally picked up the duffel bag from the baggage claim and headed, not to another airline ticket counter, but to the exit.

Davey was fitfully asleep, hanging over Brody's shoulder like a limp sack of potatoes. Eva looked flushed and glassy-eyed, as she dragged herself along beside Angeline, who *felt* flushed and glassy eyed.

She honestly didn't feel like she could even string two coherent thoughts together, as she—keeping an instinctive grip on Eva's hand—blindly followed Brody onto a small shuttle van outside the airport. Even though the van was empty and they could each have had their own long seat, they sat three abreast, with Davey still on Brody's lap.

Angeline thought it was morning, but she couldn't be certain. Her eyes felt like there were glass shards in them from lack of sleep. She couldn't even be sure where they were.

"Almost there," Brody murmured beside her.

She jerked a little, realizing her head had been sinking down onto his shoulder in the same way that Eva's head had found her lap.

The shuttle driver—a middle-aged man wearing a John Deere ball cap and a grin—looked over his shoulder at them. "You folks look like you've had a long trip. This the front end of your trip or the back?"

"Back," Brody said, his drawl an exact imitation of the driver's. "Took the family to Hawaii." He shook his head, sounding rueful. "Damn glad to be back on my own turf, if you know what I mean."

The driver chuckled. "Yessir, I do." He turned into a long-term parking lot.

Angeline would have smiled at the irony, too, if she'd had the energy. Seemed as if Hawaii was one of the very few States in which they hadn't managed to cross over or land.

The shuttle stopped and let them off, and Angeline braced herself against the weight as Brody transferred Davey to her arms. "Wait here," he said.

Angeline wouldn't have had the gumption to *not* wait. She braced her feet apart, holding the boy in her arms while Eva leaned heavily against her side and watched Brody disappear down a row of parked cars. Within minutes, a dark-colored SUV stopped beside them.

Brody came around and lifted Davey out of her arms again and strapped him into one of the rear seats. Angeline helped Eva in after her brother before taking the front seat beside Brody. She fumbled with the seat belt and he pushed her fingers away, clicking it into place himself.

"Don't worry," he murmured. "I *own* this one."

She blinked, trying to find the sense in his words. "Really?"

"Would I lie?" His hand brushed down her cheek and she felt herself pressing into his warm palm.

"Yes."

He made a soft sound. "Hang in there, toots. We'll be home soon."

"I don't even know where we are."

"Billings."

"I thought we were heading to Wyoming."

"We are."

"Then why'd we land in Montana?"

His hand finally left her cheek. "Because that's where this was." He patted the steering wheel.

"You always keep a truck parked in the long-term lot in Billings?"

"Pretty much." He sounded remarkably cheerful considering that he had to be just as tired as she was.

"It'll take us hours to get to Weaver from here."

"I never said we were going to Weaver."

She forced her eyes wider at that. They had already left the airport behind. "When you said Wyoming, I assumed—"

"Wrong."

Her lips compressed. She couldn't believe the wave of disappointment that seemed to engulf her. She'd wanted to go back to Weaver. Far more than she'd realized until knowing that it wasn't, in fact, where they were heading at all. "I should have known enough by now to ask you exactly what your intentions were."

"My intentions are always honorable," he assured, looking amused.

She closed her eyes and turned her head, resting it against the seat.

"I have a place near Sheridan," he said.

That brought her eyes right open again. She looked at him, lost for words.

"Nobody knows about it. I mean nobody who can connect it to me and what I do. We'll be safe there until I can figure out…everything."

"Oh," she managed faintly. "Is it really yours?"

"The truck or the place?"

"Both."

"Yeah. They're both really mine."

She swallowed. Moistened her lips. "So what, um, what name does it say on the ownership papers?"

"Does it matter?"

Did it? She felt oddly close to tears and blamed it on exhaustion. "No," she lied. "As long as there is an immoveable horizontal surface to sleep on, I don't much care."

"What if I told you there was no furniture?"

"Is there a floor?"

He laughed softly. "Yes."

"Then we're good to go," she murmured and closed her eyes again. Keeping them open simply took too much effort.

She didn't open them again until the shuddering of the SUV jarred her awake.

They weren't still pelting down the mountain after St. Agnes. They weren't still racing toward Venezuela. She wasn't still inhaling Brody's entire being in that heavenly hotel suite that had been overrun with bugs of an electronic variety.

"Honey, we're home." Brody singsonged in his low, deep voice. He turned off the engine and they sat there for a moment, the utter silence broken only by Davey's soft, snuffling snores.

Angeline's curiosity would kick in before long, she knew. But just then all she felt was utter relief at the sight of a long stone-fronted ranch house that sat in the crook of a small hill, with nothing but open field currently covered in undulating waves of green lying around it for nearly as far as the eye could see.

"You planning to sit here for the rest of the day?"

She realized that Brody was watching her curiously. He'd unhooked his seat belt and his door was open. Fresh air was pouring into the SUV. "No." She unsnapped her safety belt and climbed out of the truck, stretching hugely.

There was an entrance to the house on this side. Just a plain door painted a warm ivory to match the other painted portions of the structure. Those were minimal at best; most of the house was faced in rustic stone.

Brody hadn't needed to wake Davey. The boy was already climbing the concrete steps that led up to that side door. He tried the latch, and looked back at the truck. "It's locked, Mr. Dad."

"Yup." Brody took the steps in a couple bounds. He didn't pull out a key, though, she noticed. Instead, he flipped up an invisible panel near the door, punched in something, and then closed the panel up once again. "Try it now."

Davey turned the knob. The door swung open without a sound. "Cool," he breathed, and without a second's hesitation, headed inside.

"Should you let him go on ahead like that?"

"This is about the only place that I feel confident to let him explore. He's a kid." Brody shrugged. "Let him go adventuring when he can."

Something soft and sweet curled inside of her. "You'd make a good father," she murmured.

His eyebrows shot up into the brown hair that tumbled, unkempt, across his forehead. "Perish the thought." He practically shuddered as he followed the boy inside.

Soft and sweet turned crisp and dry.

She reached behind her and joggled Eva's knee. "Hey there, sweetie. Rise and shine."

Eva slowly peeled open one weary eye,

and the girl fairly tumbled out of the truck. Angeline caught her arm, and together they made their way up the steps and inside.

Not knowing what to expect about the interior—maybe all he really did have were bare floors and unfurnished rooms, after all—the sight that greeted them came as a welcome surprise.

The door they'd come in through opened onto a tidy, slightly austere laundry room. On one side was another door, open to reveal a half bath, and on the other was a kitchen that could have popped from the pages of a decorating magazine. Lots of gleaming granite countertop and stainless steel appliances built into warm wood cabinets.

Off to one side, surrounded by a bay of windows that overlooked the—her tired mind tried to orient herself—the rear of the property, she decided, sat a large square walnut table, surrounded by four chairs. It even held a wooden bowl of fruit in the center of it.

From overhead, she could hear the faint thump of rapid footsteps. Undoubtedly Davey's as he continued his intrepid exploration. She followed Eva from the kitchen into a hallway that wasn't really a hall at all

but more of an open circle. The staircase—
pretty much a masterpiece of carved
wood—curved up the wall to the second
floor. There were a few closed doors and the
other side of the round area opened into a
giant great room.

The house *definitely* didn't look so large
from the outside.

Davey popped his head over the landing
above them. "Eva, come *see*. There's a room
for you and a room for me."

Showing a little more life, Eva went up the
stairs to join her brother.

Angeline crossed the great room, drawn by
the view from the windows on the far wall
of the not-so-distant mountains. Something
about that view had everything inside her
seeming to sigh in relief and missing Weaver.

"Come on."

She looked over her shoulder. Standing
amid the collection of leather couches and
nubby upholstered chairs, Brody looked surprisingly "in" place. Which made her realize
that she'd never let herself think about
whether or not the man even *had* a home.
He'd always been just "Brody"—an entire
entity, complete and intact all on his own—

as if he had no need or desire for the usual things that most people wanted in their lives.

"Where?"

"You wanted a horizontal surface, didn't you?"

The thought that swept into her mind had absolutely nothing to do with the act of sleeping upon one. She tucked her tongue behind her teeth and nodded. "Sleep." The word sounded forced.

And if the way Brody's lips twitched was any indication, he was well aware of the direction of her unruly thoughts. He turned, but instead of heading toward the staircase, he opened one of the doors in that circular nonhallway, and waited, clearly expecting Angeline to precede him.

She passed through the doorway and went a little limp inside at the perfection of the master suite that waited on the other side. At least she assumed it was the master suite. As a guest bedroom, it would definitely border on overkill.

The bed was massive, owing a good portion of that impression to the rich, deep gleam of the wooden bed frame. The mattress was even covered with a thoroughly un-bachelor-like comforter. All golds and reds and browns that were complemented by co-ordinating pillows—again oversized and beautiful without managing to be frilly or fussy. The tall narrow windows that flanked the bed were dressed with wooden shutters, currently open, and cornices over the top finished with fabric that matched the bedding. There were two chairs sitting alongside each other in another corner with a table tucked between. The perfect spot for coffee in the morning. Aside from them, there was no other freestanding furniture in the room at all. Everything else—shelves and drawers—was constructed of wood that looked similar to the bed and was built into the wall facing it. And in the center of all that detailed woodwork was a fireplace. One of the most perfectly beautiful fireplaces she'd ever seen.

"Who, um, who did the decorating for you?"

He looked wounded. "What? You think I couldn't have done it?"

She walked to the fireplace and reached up to pluck a fat, squat red candle off the mantel. She sniffed it. "You picked out bayberry candles?"

His dimple flashed. "Okay. I hired an outfit to take care of things for me. They *did* follow my instructions," he added defensively. "Do you think I have no taste whatsoever?"

She sat on the edge of the bed and the mattress was so high that her toes actually cleared the floor. "I think," she said slowly, "that I don't really know you at all. I thought I did, but…" She shook her head, her voice trailing away.

He stood with his back to the fireplace. Above the mantel with its artful collection of candles and an engraved wooden box, a large oil painting of a handsome couple posed with two small children was propped against the stone chimney. "But now you don't? What is it you want to know?"

What *did* she want to know? Besides everything?

She looked from Brody's face to the family portrait. There wasn't really a resemblance that she could spot between the faces there and his, but what other purpose would he have for displaying it in his private bedroom if they were strangers?

She realized she was pressing her thumb against the wedding ring that she still hadn't taken off her finger, turning it in a slow circle. "How long have you lived here?" It wasn't at all the deep, meaningful questions that plagued her where he was concerned.

"I had this house built nearly five years ago."

More surprises. For some reason she'd had the sense he'd acquired it more recently. "Built," she said slowly. "But how *long* have you lived here?"

He smiled faintly. "About six months, give or take. I…made more permanent arrangements to be here when I was pulling the gig in Weaver last November."

He meant when he was protecting little Megan.

"Why then?"

He lifted a shoulder. "I was in the vicinity. Easier to take care of the details."

"No. I mean *why* then? If you hadn't really lived here in all the time since you built it, what prompted you to do something about it in November?"

His lashes narrowed. His blue eyes were bloodshot and his jaw was shaded with whiskers. His jeans seemed to hang a little loosely on his tight hips and the blue shirt was definitely looking travel weary.

She could only imagine what state his bandage was in.

He looked, frankly, like hell, yet he was still the most beautiful man she'd ever seen.

"That's not really a question you want to be asking right now," he said.

She shifted, pressing her palms flat on the mattress beside her hips. "Why?" Her voice turned wry. "Don't I have a high enough security clearance to hear the details?"

"No. Because everything I've ever done about this place has been prompted by you."

Chapter Thirteen

Brody's words swirled inside Angeline's head, making her dizzy. Or maybe it was her heart, shuddering around inside without an even beat to save its soul, that was causing her curious light-headededness.

How could *she* have ever influenced something in Brody's personal life?

They'd barely known one another.

That didn't stop you from falling for him.

She ignored the voice inside her head. Moistened her lips and swallowed against the sudden constriction there. "I don't understand."

He rubbed his chin, looking oddly uneasy. And when, less than a moment later, Davey bolted into the room, he looked happy for the interruption.

He leaned over and scooped the boy up by the waist, leaving his arms and legs dangling.

Davey gave a squeal of laughter and squirmed.

Angeline's heart lurched all over again. She looked from Brody and the boy to the portrait once more.

"Where's your sister?" Brody was asking the giggling boy.

"In the bathroom," Davey managed to impart between laughs. "*Again.*" He tried to reach Brody's torso with his little fingers, intent on tickling, but couldn't. "Are we gonna stay here until my mom and dad come to get us?"

"That's the plan. Which means we've got to get some food into this place so we don't starve." Brody swung the boy from one side to the other.

Davey went into peals of laughter again.

Clearly, *he* wasn't upset by the latest turn of events.

Angeline pushed herself off the bed,

ignoring the weak feeling that still plagued her knees, and started for the doorway.

"Where you going?"

"To figure out what you need in your kitchen."

He shook his head, waving away the idea. "No need. I'll just call up Mrs. Bedford."

"Who's that?" Davey asked curiously, beating Angeline to the punch.

"She," Brody swung the kid upright finally, and brought their noses close, "is my housekeeper," he told him. "And she'll have us set up with plenty of food in just two shakes."

"Two shakes of what?"

"Of you." Brody jiggled the boy again, sending him into another spasm of laughter.

Angeline smiled faintly, as entranced by the unguarded grin on Brody's face as she was by the idea that Brody had something as unlikely as a housekeeper. "I'll just make sure the kids get settled in, then," she said.

"Take a nap," Brody told her, nodding toward the bed. His bed. "I can handle them on my own for a bit."

She pressed her lips together. The truth was, after the last few days she believed that Brody was capable of handling them for a lot more than a "bit." He wasn't just good at protecting children. No matter how much he shuddered over the idea of having his own, he was good *with* children.

It shamed her that she was so surprised by the fact. As if she'd given him short shrift when she—coming from the family that she did—should know just exactly how multifaceted a caring man could be.

"Maybe I should use one of the other rooms," she suggested.

Davey had looped his arm around Brody's shoulder. "But then I'd gotta share with Eva. And I *al-ays* gotta share with her."

Brody's gaze slanted toward Angeline, full of sudden devilry. "Think of his sacrifice, babe. We can't have that."

She swallowed. *That* was the Brody she knew and loved.

Unfortunately, she was well aware that thought had become less a turn of phrase than reality with every passing hour they'd spent together.

"Fine." She headed back toward the bed, watching Brody from the corner of her eyes as she slowly reached for one of the large, decorative pillows at the head of it. She pushed it aside, and turned back the comforter, revealing the smooth chocolate-brown sheets beneath.

He suddenly looked less goading and more…disconcerted. "All right then. Let's leave her to it, Dave, my man." He tossed the boy over his shoulder, setting off more giggles, and headed to the door. When Angeline caught him looking back at her, she deliberately drew back the top sheet and sat down on the bed. She leaned back and slowly toed off one boot. Then the other.

Brody shook his head. "You're dangerous," he muttered, and closed the door on her, leaving her alone in the room.

She flopped back on the bed, her palm pressed to her thundering heart. What was dangerous was thinking that she could ever play with the fire that was Brody Paine and come out unscorched.

She rolled over, tucking the down bed pillow that had been hidden behind the sham beneath her cheek, and wondered how many nights—and with how many women—Brody had spent in the wide, comfortable bed.

Her gaze slid to the portrait yet again.

Whatever had come before didn't necessarily matter, she knew. Because she was only there as a result of the Stanley situation.

She'd do well to remember that particular fact.

Then she deliberately closed her eyes. If she didn't sleep, she'd at least pretend to.

But it wasn't long before pretense became reality. When next Angeline opened her eyes, there was nothing but moonlight shining through the opened shutters.

The fat pillows had all been removed from the bed and were sitting, stacked haphazardly on the two chairs by the other windows. The comforter had been pulled back across the bed, as if it had been shoved aside by a tall, warm body.

The evidence that Brody, too, must have slept at some point right there beside her made something inside her heat. And it wasn't at all the uneasy kind of feeling she'd had when they'd shared that narrow mattress at St. Agnes.

Now, though, there as no sign of him.

She rolled onto her back, stretching luxuriously. She felt quite refreshed, even given the fact that she'd been sleeping fully dressed. She pushed off the bed and padded across the thick rug that covered much of the hardwood floors and went into the adjoining bathroom.

As appealing as soaking herself in hot bubbling water sounded, she contented herself with a shower instead, dragging the opaque burgundy and gold striped curtain around the circular rod that hung over the tub. The water was hot and plentiful and was almost as welcoming as Brody's bed had been. She used his soap, which smelled like some sort of spicy forest, and his shampoo, which smelled like babies and made her want to giggle.

Brody Paine used baby shampoo on that thick sandy hair of his.

Finally, feeling squeaky clean for the first time in days, she turned off the water and yanked back the curtain.

Brody was sitting there on the closed commode facing the tub.

She yelped and grabbed the edge of the curtain, dragging it across her torso. Her face felt flushed, and her body felt even hotter. "What on earth are you doing?" He'd obviously showered, too, because his hair was still damp and he'd exchanged his blue jeans and blue T-shirt for clean ones, this time both in black.

"Hey," he defended. "I'm covering my eyes."

He was. With one hand that she didn't trust in the least spread across the upper portion of his face.

She slowly let the curtain drop, almost but not quite revealing her nipples that had gone appallingly tight at the unexpected sight of him, and twisted her lips when the coffee cup he was holding nearly spilled right onto his lap. "As I suspected," she said, managing a tart tone only through sheer effort.

He dropped the hand and extended the coffee toward her. "I was just thinking of you," he drawled.

She shoved the edge of the curtain beneath her arms holding it tight there, and reached for the white mug. Less than a week ago, she would have dismissed his words as pure blarney.

Now, after all the things he'd done, said, she was no longer sure about anything.

She sipped at the coffee, hot, fragrant and strong just how she liked it, and eyed him. His feet were bare and that, more than anything—even her barely protected nudity— made her feel shaky inside.

They were so intimate, she realized.

Those bare feet of his. Lightly dusted with dark hair. High arches. Long, vaguely knobby toes. She pressed her lips together for a moment. "Did you keep your bandage dry when you showered?" The words sort of blurted out of her.

His lips tilted. "I put a brand new one on, ma'am."

She could only imagine the results of that, given the first bandage she'd witnessed. "Where are the children?"

"Snug as bugs in their beds."

"What about supper? Did they eat? I should probably check—"

He lifted his head, cutting off her litany. "I fixed them mac and cheese. Evidently not some fried variety that Davey thinks is the bomb, but it filled their stomachs. At least his. Eva did more picking than anything. They had baths, a few minutes of television and then they had bed. Only thing they didn't have was a story read to them by yours truly," he added drily. "Satisfied?"

She narrowed her eyes at him. "What time is it now?"

"Almost eight. And no, that isn't decaf in case you're about ready to ask that, too."

"I wasn't. I would never make the mistake of thinking you might let a little thing like caffeine stop you, even at eight o'clock at night. Um," she gestured with the mug toward the towels hanging on the wall opposite him. "Mind handing me a towel?"

He hooked a long toffee-colored towel off the rod and held it out to her. She exchanged the mug for the towel, careful to remain behind the protection of the curtain as she dashed it over her wet limbs before wrapping it sarong-wise around her, tucking the ends in above her breasts. "Any luck reaching your handler?"

"Not exactly."

She peeked out from the curtain again. "What does that mean?"

"I reached someone," he said. "The situation hasn't changed."

Which could mean anything, she supposed, but since he wasn't looking like they needed to bug out, she'd follow his lead. "It's, um, it's pretty rude of you to just bust in like this, you know. Didn't your parents teach you some manners?"

"My parents were British. They were *all* about manners," he assured. His gaze drifted downward, from her wet hair to her hands clutching the shielding curtain. "Why are you still a virgin?"

She stared at him. The porcelain of the tub was losing its heat without the water pounding on it, and her toes curled against the slick surface. "I thought we agreed that was none of your business."

"It wasn't." He leaned forward, his hands folded loosely between his knees, looking thoroughly casual. As if he held conversations like this in his bathroom most every day. "Now it is."

"*Now?* Why now?"

His casual mien abruptly slipped and her mouth dried at the hunger darkening his eyes. "Because the plan to keep my hands off you isn't going to work much longer."

No amount of effort seemed enough to propel a single word past her lips.

He pushed to his feet. "Do you really think I make a habit of busting in, uninvited, on women in the shower? That I don't know how the bloody hell to wait for an invite?"

She swallowed. "Brody," she whispered.

"So you'd better tell me *why,* love, and make it a good one while you're at it." He stopped when his legs encountered the side

of the tub. "One that even my damned conscience can manage to heed."

She sucked in a breath. Moistened her lips.
And still nothing emerged but his name.
Husky. Soft.

His eyes darkened even more, the blue
looking nearly as black as the shirt stretched
across his wide shoulders. "That's not helping
me any here, Angeline. Are you waiting for
marriage? For—" his mobile lips twisted
slightly "—hell, I don't know. True love?"

She lifted her chin. "Something wrong
with that?"

He muttered an oath. "I should have known."

She slicked her hand over her hair, pushing
the tangles behind her ear. "I just never...
trusted anyone enough to believe they cared
all that much about me. About what was
behind," she waved her hand, feeling herself
flush. "You know. Behind the genetics. The
looks. The, um, the—"

"Body?"

She nodded, feeling foolish.

"I'm sorry to break it to you, babe, but
you've got more than your share of both
going on," he murmured.

She pressed her lips together. "So men

have been telling me since I was barely a teenager. All I ever heard were catcalls and wolf whistles by the idiots. The nice guys, well, they didn't ever call because they figured I was already out living it up, or they didn't want to get turned down. Leaving Weaver didn't help. If anything, it got worse."

She flinched a little when Brody's hand came up and touched her shoulder.

The hunger was still in his eyes, but it was the gentleness in his touch that stole her breath all over again. "And I behaved the same way."

She sank her teeth into her lip. "S-sometimes."

"It was the only way I knew how to keep you at arm's length," he murmured. "You think I didn't know that flirting with you was the quickest road to keeping things simple where you were concerned? That I didn't recognize the stop signs that always came up in those brown eyes of yours?" His thumb traced a slow circle around her shoulder. "I needed those signs, Angeline."

The edge of the curtain wrinkled even more in her tight grip. "Why?"

His thumb slowly, so slowly, dragged down her arm toward her elbow. "Because being with you made me want things I gave up wanting a long time ago." He reached her wrist and stopped, resting over the vein that pulsed there. "You remember when we first met?"

"I could hardly forget."

"You told me about Wyoming. And everything about you—inside here—" he let go of her wrist long enough to tap the center of her forehead "—and here," he drew his finger in a short, burning line from the base of her throat to her cleavage that wasn't exactly hidden by the thick folds of towel tucked there, "shined out like a homing beacon."

He looked up at the curtain hanging from the rod, and seemed to study it for a moment. "I always thought it was interesting that you'd chosen to go to Atlanta considering the way you always talked about Wyoming. For a long time, I figured that it must have had something to do with a man."

She shook her head. "I was just sticking close to my sister. We missed each other."

"I know how that feels." His gaze slowly dropped again, still studying the curtain, only this time where she held it gripped in her fist. "I bought this land shortly after you and I met and had the house built within less than a year. And I've already told you I started actually living here late last year." He breathed out a half laugh. "Not because I ever expected us to be standing here like this someday, that's for certain."

She waited for his low voice to continue, barely daring to breathe. "Then why?"

"Because I wanted to feel what you felt that first day we met. I wanted to see if I *could*. If it was still in me, or if it had been burned out of me when I was still a kid."

Her eyes went damp. "What happened, Brody? Or is it really Simon after all?"

"It used to be," he murmured. "But it doesn't matter anymore."

The curtain slipped in her loosened grip. "Of course it matters. It's your past." The portrait over his fireplace hung in her mind's eye. "You had a sister. What was her name?"

"Penelope. Penny."

"What happened to her?"

He shook his head. "This isn't about my past. This is about why you've chosen to remain a virgin."

"I think," she began softly, cautiously, "that this is about both." She let the curtain fall away between them. "You want me to give you an inviolate reason why I've never slept with a man. One that will convince you once and for all that I'm off-limits. Not because you're worried that I might be compromising some deeply held belief about sex before marriage or any of that. But because you're afraid that it wouldn't *be* just sex. Because it might open that door on emotions that you like to keep closed because if you don't," her voice was strained, "everything that you've been able to pretend no longer affected you will come tumbling down on you. Like one of those closets that people keep shoving stuff into, again and again and again only to find, one day, they forget themselves and open the door and—" she waved her hand "—whoosh. There are all our issues piled up, nice and unresolved, around our ears."

"Maybe," he countered, "I just like a woman with more experience."

She shook her head and slowly stepped out of the tub. "Are you expecting that to hurt?" Level on the floor with him, she had to tilt her head back to keep her eyes on his. "To push me away? It might work if I believed you. Maybe," she lifted her hands and settled them softly on his chest, "you just feel safer with a woman who doesn't make you feel anything."

His eyes narrowed. He caught her wrists in his hands as if to pull them away from him. "Brave words," he cautioned.

She didn't feel particularly brave. She felt out on a limb in every possible way. "Prove me wrong, then," she whispered.

His jaw seemed to tighten as she twisted her wrists out of his light hold. She reached for the towel and flipped the knot loose.

The towel dropped to her bare feet.

He exhaled roughly. "Thought you were all about playing by the rules."

She stepped out from the folds of terry, closing the last few inches remaining between them, almost but not quite smiling when the man actually took a step back.

"And you're the one who thinks rules were just made to be broken." She inched forward again, until her bare toes touched his, and her breasts brushed the soft fabric of his T-shirt.

"I don't want the thing that gets broken to be you."

There were already too many emotions swirling inside her to examine the way his rough admission made her want to cry, as much for him as for her. "I'm a big girl," she assured softly. She slid her hand behind his neck, tugging his head toward hers. "All grown up."

"I didn't have any doubts about that." His assurance murmured against her lips and his hands finally came around her back, pressing warm and hot against her spine.

She still shivered, but not with cold.

Not when his body felt like a furnace burning through his clothes to her flesh. Not when her blood seemed to expand inside her veins and her nerve endings set off sparks wherever he touched.

"You deserve a bed," he muttered, his mouth dragging down the column of her throat. "Some romance or something. Not tedious flights and questionable hotels."

"This isn't a hotel." She sucked in a harsh breath when his hands dragged over her hips, his fingers kneading. "I'll reserve judgment on the questionable part for now, if you don't mind."

He laughed softly and pulled her right off her feet, until her mouth met his. His hands slid down her thighs, pulling them around his waist, and he carried her out of the bathroom into the bedroom.

She swung her legs down when he stopped next to the bed. He pressed his forehead to hers for a long moment, then shook his head a little, straightening. His fingers threaded through the wet skeins of her hair, spreading it out past her shoulders. "I can't not tell you that you're beautiful," he murmured. "Because you are."

She swallowed. His hands drifted from her shoulders, skimmed over the full jut of her breasts only to stop and torment the hard crests into even tighter points, while need shot through her veins, all collecting in the center of her until she felt weak from it.

Her fingers flexed, desperate for something more substantial to grab on to than air. She satisfied them with handfuls of his shirt that she dragged loose from the waist of his jeans. "What did you do with Delilah?"

He snorted. "You want to know that *now?* God, I am getting old."

She finally got her hands beneath his shirt, and ran them up his long spine, swept out over his wide back. "I've wondered ever since we left San Juan," she murmured.

"I left her with Roger. Compensation for the bugs of his I drowned." He caught her waist again and covered her mouth, kissing any more silly questions she might have uttered into nonexistence.

She pulled in gulps of air when he finally lifted his head.

"Anything else you want to discuss?"

She pushed his shirt higher and he finally yanked it off over his head. As she'd suspected, the bandage he'd covered himself with was almost as much a disaster as the first one had been.

She vowed to change it for him. Later.

She slid her fingers through his, pulling his hands boldly back to her breasts. "Does this feel as good to you as it does to me?"

"That'll take further examination." He dragged his thumbs over and around, again and again as he backed her inexorably against the side of the bed until, off balanced, she tumbled backward.

He must have turned on the lamp near the chairs while she'd been in the shower, because it hadn't been burning when she'd wakened. Now, she was glad for its soft glow as he stood there above her, his eyes dark and full of intent. He undid his jeans and pushed them off, and Angeline let her eyes take their glorious fill.

"*I* can't not tell you you're beautiful," she whispered huskily and slowly lifted her hand toward him.

The mattress dipped when he bent his knee against it. He took her hand, pressed his mouth to the palm of it. Her other hand found his hip, drifted over the unbelievably hard glute that flexed in answer to her touch.

He suddenly grabbed that exploratory hand and pressed it, along with the other above her head.

Her breath came faster, so much emotion rocketing around inside her that she thought she might burst. "What about your chest? I don't want you to undo whatever healing has already occurred."

"If my heart can withstand this, I think that damn knife wound can," he muttered, and pressed his mouth to the pulse beating wildly at the base of her throat. "I could spend a lifetime exploring you."

"I don't want to wait that long," she assured, twining her legs impatiently around his, trying to pull him down to her. She knew he wanted her. There was no hiding that particularly evident, impressive, fact.

"For a virgin, you're quite the demanding

little thing, aren't you?" He dropped his mouth even farther, exploring the rise of her breasts.

"Brody—" She pressed her head back in the soft bedding, writhing against his tormenting tongue.

"That's my name," he whispered, as he continued southward. "Feel free to wear it out." And when his mouth reached her *there,* and everything inside her splintered outward, she was afraid she well might, as she cried out his name. Again. And again.

Tears streaked from her eyes when he finally worked his way back up her trembling body. "Now," he said, his body settling in the cradle of her thighs. "Are you sure?"

She arched against him, winding herself around him and answered the question once and for all as she took him into her body. "God," he gritted, "Angeline."

"That's my name," she returned breathlessly, full of wonder. Full of him. "Feel free to—"

He pulled her more tightly beneath him, and the words died in her throat as heat and pleasure and everything that was right and beautiful in the world came screaming together in the collision of their bodies. And when that pleasure was more than she could bear yet again and she exploded apart in his arms, he groaned her name, following her headlong into the fire.

Eventually, when their hearts finally stopped pounding against each other, he lifted his head.

He looked just as undone as she felt and she sighed softly. Contentedly. "You were worth the wait," she whispered.

His eyes darkened. He slowly kissed her lips.

Then he looked over at the portrait across from the bed that they'd nearly destroyed. "I was born in London. They named me Simon Brody," he murmured. "After him. Until I was fifteen and I learned otherwise, I thought he was my father. Only it turns out that my mother didn't meet Simon until Penny was two and my mother was pregnant with me. They married right after I was born."

She curled her arms around him and his head lowered to her breast. "How did you find out?"

"I found my birth certificate. I was grounded for smoking and bored, so I was snooping. I never expected to find *that*."

"I learned a long time ago that it doesn't take blood for a man to be a father. Did you love him?"

He was silent for so long that she wasn't sure he'd answer. She sifted her fingers slowly through his hair and finally, he did. "Yes."

"Then that's all that matters, Brody. Love is always the thing that matters most."

His hand slid down and caught hers. She knew he felt the wedding ring that she still hadn't bothered to remove. And when he folded her fingers in his, and kissed them, she couldn't stop herself from wishing—just for a moment—that the ring was real.

Chapter Fourteen

"Mr. Dad. Angeline."

The voice was faint, but Angeline sat bolt upright and nearly screamed when she heard a crash from some distant part of the house.

"Stay here." Beside her, Brody was already pushing back the covers. He stopped only long enough to hitch his jeans over his hips and pull something from a hidden panel in the wall as he left the room.

Angeline scrambled out of bed, nearly tripping over the tangle of bedding they'd made. She fumbled her way into the scrubs that were the first thing her hands encountered in the duffel she'd yet to unpack. Her heart was in her throat, waiting for God knew what.

Another cry from Davey?

Another crash?

A gunshot?

Heedless of Brody's instruction, she headed out of the room, stopping short at the panel that was still open. With only the lamp on the far side of the room as her guide, she peered into the wall safe. Stuck her hand in, sweeping it around the walls inside.

Even in the dark hole of the safe, she recognized what her fingers found. Guns. And plenty of them.

She closed her palm around one grip and pulled it off the bracket holding it in place and stuck her head out the bedroom door that Brody had left ajar.

All she heard was the banging of her heartbeat inside her head.

Could Santina's thug have found them even after all their precautions?

She quietly padded across the floor toward the base of the staircase.

"Angeline."

She nearly jumped out of her skin at the sound of Brody calling her name. Loudly.

"What is it? What's wrong?" She started up the stairs.

"Eva's sick. She's burning up." He met her in the hallway and muttered an oath when he saw the gun she held. "Give me that."

He plucked it out of her unresisting hand and Angeline dashed into the room. Davey was huddled at the foot of the bed, looking scared. Eva was curled up in a fetal position, and was definitely fevered. The heat practically rolled off her in waves.

Angeline sat down beside her. "Honey, how long have you felt like this?" She surreptitiously found Eva's wrist and felt her pulse.

"I dunno." The girl shifted away, as if she couldn't bear the touch. "My stomach hurts," she added hoarsely, and promptly threw up across Angeline's lap.

Davey jumped back. "Eeuuww." But he sounded more tearful than anything.

"Run in the bathroom across the hall and grab the towels," Brody told Davey.

The boy dashed out of the room.

"She needs the hospital," Angeline said, looking up at Brody. Everything inside her felt seized up by guilt as she cradled the girl against her. She'd slept the day away after they'd arrived, and after that, she and Brody had—

She shied away from thinking about the hours spent in his arms.

"This could be anything from a bug she's picked up to appendicitis," she told him.

"Here." Davey returned with the towels tumbling out of his arms.

Brody took one and gave it back to him. "Go get this one really wet." Again the boy dashed out and Brody, without turning a single hair, began mopping up the mess.

"I'm sorry," Eva cried.

Angeline lifted the girl's dark hair out of the way for Brody. "Nothing for you to be sorry about, sweetie." She, on the other hand, had plenty. If she'd been paying more atten- tion to the children and less to Brody—

"I want my mom."

Angeline's eyes burned. "I know you do, Eva. She'd be here too, if she could." She took the soaked towel that Davey came back with and smoothed the corner of it over Eva's flushed face. "I want to get you out of these pj's, okay?" The pajamas in question were comprised of the same scrub shirt that Eva had worn in Caracas and Angeline drew it over the girl's head.

Brody added it to the soiled sheets that he'd managed to slide out from beneath Angeline and Eva.

One portion of Angeline's mind wondered how many times he'd had to deal with vomiting children because he was more than a little adept at it.

"All she's got left that are clean are jeans." He was staring into the top drawer of the bureau. "No way are you getting those on her. I'll grab a shirt of mine." He headed out of the room, though she could easily hear his voice as he went. "Come on, Davey. You better get your shoes on so we can take your sister to the doctor."

"Is she gonna be okay?"

"Heck, yeah. You think Angeline and I would let anything happen to either one of you?"

She bit her lip. She wished she felt that sort of confidence. That she *deserved* that sort of confidence. "I'm going to have Brody carry you down to the car when he gets back, okay?"

Eva nodded slightly. "What if I throw up again?"

"Then you do." Angeline pressed her lips to the girl's sweaty forehead. "It's not the end of the world." Brody came back into the room a few minutes later. Not only did he bring a T-shirt for Eva, but one for Angeline, as well as her jeans and boots.

While he helped Eva maneuver into the shirt, Angeline hurriedly exchanged her ruined scrubs for the clean clothes.

"You finish dressing. I'm going to take her down to the truck." Brody gingerly lifted the girl into his arms and headed out of the bedroom.

Angeline fumbled with the boots, only to realize he'd tucked socks inside them.

And he'd accused *her* of getting caught up in details.

She pulled them on, shoved her feet into the boots and hurriedly caught up to them on the staircase where Davey was already waiting, clinging to the banister. Angeline took his hand and within minutes they were in the SUV, racing away from the house.

Fortunately, when they reached the town, traffic at that hour was nil and they arrived at the hospital in short order. Brody pulled right up in the emergency entrance by the door and carried Eva inside. Angeline barely managed to pull the keys from the ignition before she and Davey followed.

The waiting room was empty and with one look at Eva's condition, the nurse standing by the reception desk waved Brody through a set of double doors behind her.

"Use the passport," Brody told Angeline before the doors closed between them.

She blinked.

"Ma'am? I'll need you to complete just a few things and you can go back with your husband and daughter."

She focused in on the receptionist who was holding a pen and clipboard out toward her. "Right." As a paramedic, she ought to have been intimately familiar with the process of checking in a patient through the E.R., yet she really wasn't. Their end of the paperwork was considerably different than the patient's end.

So she scribbled one of her names of the day—Angie Black—where the receptionist pointed, and filled in the only address that her frantic mind could remember—the one she'd grown up with in Weaver. "We, um, we just moved here," she told the receptionist, as if that would explain her complete and utter inadequacy when it came to answering the simple questions.

Beside her, Davey was standing on his tiptoes, trying to see over the desk. "Where'd Mr. Dad and my sister go?"

The reception smiled at the term. Angeline supposed she must have heard just about anything and everything in her position. "They went back to have the doctor look at your sister and see what he can do to make her feel better." The woman produced a plastic-wrapped sucker and handed it over. "It's sugar free," she assured Angeline.

Davey didn't let that bother him as he whipped off the plastic and started sucking on it.

Then Brody stuck his head through the double doors. "Angeline." His head disappeared again.

She started to call Davey, but the receptionist shook her head. "Let him stay out with me," she advised. "It's a slow night. I don't mind."

Torn, Angeline looked at the boy. What was the likelihood of any harm coming to him there? "Davey, you stay right here with—" she looked toward the receptionist.

"Bonny."

"—Bonny," she repeated to Davey. "No going off and exploring, okay?"

He shrugged and sat down on one of the chairs near the television set. "Can I watch cartoons?"

"We'll find some for you," Bonny assured. "We'll pop in a videotape if need be."

Angeline hurried through the swinging doors.

There was no question where Eva had been taken because she could see Brody standing not far down the hall.

Eva was already on a hospital gurney. One nurse was drawing blood. Another was attaching an IV. And the doctor, a young man who looked old enough to be a grade schooler, introduced himself as Dr. Thomas.

He pulled the curtain shielding the bed closed somewhat and stepped out with them on the other side. "The blood test will confirm it, but I believe your daughter's appendix has decided to create a fuss. The surgeon on duty tonight is Dr. Campbell. He's already scrubbing in. We don't want to waste any time and chance it rupturing. We'll need you to sign the consent papers as soon as they're ready."

Angeline looked at Brody, lost for words. Of course she'd known it could come to this; she wasn't a fool. But knowing and doing were two very different things.

"I'll sign whatever you need," Brody said evenly. His hand closed around Angeline's shoulder. "Just make sure she's all right."

Dr. Thomas smiled reassuringly. "Better that you brought her now, than a few hours from now." He tugged back the curtain again. "Eva, the nurse is going to give you something that's going to make you really sleepy, and then we're going to get rid of that nasty pain in your tummy. Okay?"

Eva's dark eyes were tightly shut. "I wanna go home."

Angeline went to her side, closing that small fist in her hands. She pressed her lips to the girl's temple. "We all want that," she assured her. "You're going to be all right, though. A little while from now you're going to be feeling a whole lot better."

"We need to move her," one of the nurses said in a kind voice.

Angeline nodded and stepped back from the gurney. "We'll be right here waiting for you, Eva."

The dark head managed a small nod of acknowledgment.

Then the nurses were rolling the gurney quickly along the hall.

"She'll be fine," Dr. Thomas assured. "All her symptoms say there's been no rupture yet." He pushed open the doors back out to the waiting area. "Once you finish with the forms, Bonny can tell you how to get to the waiting area outside surgery. It'll be a little more comfortable for you there."

"Thanks," Brody said, turning toward Bonny and the waiting forms. He picked up the pen and with an efficiency that Angeline envied, completed the form. Then he pulled out a cell phone that he must have brought from the house, because she'd certainly never seen it before, and punched in a few numbers. "Mrs. Bedford? Simon Black here, again. I have a bit of an emergency."

Angeline started. She'd thought he'd just made up the name of Black for the purpose of the passports that Roger had produced for them. But obviously, if his housekeeper knew him by that name, he was used to using that particular alias.

"Ma'am?" Bonny drew her attention away from Brody, who was asking Mrs. Bedford if she'd mind coming to pick up Davey from the hospital. "I need your signature, as well." She held out the pen that Brody had used.

Angeline slowly took it and wrote in her name next to his. Only after she'd finished did she realize she'd not used the diminutive of Angie, but Angeline.

She eyed the names, side by side, feeling distinctly off balanced. Simon and Angeline Black.

"Okay." Brody had pocketed his phone. "Mrs. Bedford will be here shortly. Timing couldn't be better, actually. When she dropped off the groceries earlier today—all of you were snoozing like Rip Van Winkle—she had her grandson with her. Cute kid. Davey will like him."

"I can direct you to the other waiting room now if you'd like," Bonny suggested.

A short while later, they found themselves seats in the much smaller, but much more comfortable waiting room. Angeline couldn't make herself sit in one of the upholstered chairs, though, and paced slowly around the room, conscientiously giving the other couple who was also in the waiting room their space and privacy, as well.

Davey sat on Brody's lap, his blond head resting against that chest that Angeline knew from experience was wide and comforting.

Her pacing feet took her back to them. "You should get a tetanus shot while we're here," she told him.

"What's tet-nus?"

"Like a vaccine," Brody told Davey. "I had one a year ago."

"Still." Angeline paced away again. Every time she looked at the clock on the wall, she expected hours to have passed, but instead, it was only minutes.

Before too long, a woman in her fifties, Angeline guessed, arrived. "Angeline, this is Mrs. Bedford," Brody introduced them. "She's the one who keeps the house looking like the Pope himself will be dropping by any minute."

Mrs. Bedford's cheeks flushed with pleasure. "Oh, you and your teasing." She turned her bright gaze on Angeline. "We'd have met earlier but I know you were all just tuckered right out. I'm so glad I'm able to help now, though. How's the girl?"

"She's in surgery."

"Oh, my. Bless her heart. What a miracle that you were here when it happened." Mrs. Bedford sighed a little but then patted Angeline's shoulder as if she'd known her since she was a tot. "Don't you worry, though. The doctors here are just fine. Kept my Joe going when he had a heart attack a few years ago, that's for sure."

Angeline managed a smile. If she'd held any suspicion that the housekeeper might really be associated with Hollins-Winword, they pretty much dissolved in the face of her kindly ordinariness.

The woman was holding out her hand for Davey. "You can call me Mrs. B.," she told him. "How'd you like to go to my house and have some ice cream with me? My husband and my grandson, Tyson, are there, too."

Evidently, the notion of ice cream at midnight was enough to overcome whatever reservations Davey might have. He took the woman's hand and waved as he left with her.

Angeline rubbed her hands up and down her arms. "You're not worried about…you know?"

Brody shook his head. "She's more capable than you give her credit for."

Which just had Angeline wondering all over again.

She began pacing once more, only sitting next to Brody when a surgeon came in to speak to the other couple.

Judging by their devastated expressions, the news was not good.

She looked away. Brody reached over and closed his hand around hers and the urge to pace finally died.

The waiting room was empty except for them when a middle-aged man wearing a white coat over green scrubs entered and looked around. "Mr. and Mrs. Black?"

Angeline and Brody rose from their chairs. She swallowed, and felt Brody's hand slide around her shoulders. "That's us," he said.

Angeline tried and failed to decipher the man's expression as he crossed the waiting room toward them. Her stomach felt tight, her nerves shredded.

"I'm Dr. Campbell," he introduced himself without preamble. "Eva's surgery went very well. She's doing fine."

The relief was nearly overwhelming. Angeline's knees started to shake. Brody held her even tighter, as if he were trying to lend some strength to her.

"We got the appendix before it ruptured," Dr. Campbell was saying, "which is a very good thing. Her recovery time should be minimal."

"When can we see her?"

"She'll be moved from the recovery room to her own room within the next hour or so. Go get yourselves some coffee. Something to eat. Stretch your legs. That'll help take up the time," he advised, "until she's settled in her room. Unless you have any questions?" He lifted his eyebrows.

Angeline had a million of them, but couldn't seem to marshal her thoughts enough to voice a single one.

And Brody was decidedly silent, as well.

The surgeon didn't seem to notice anything amiss in their reactions, though. As if he were used to it. "I'll be along to check on her again in a few hours. We can talk then, too. And of course you can call at any time. Just ask one of the nurses."

"Thank you."

Brody stuck out his hand, shaking the surgeon's before the man walked back out of the waiting room.

Angeline sank down onto the edge of the chair, pressing her fingertips to her forehead. "This is all my fault." If she'd paid more attention to Eva she might have realized that the girl was suffering from more than just worry over her parents. "She's probably been working on this for days."

"Whether she was or not, it's hardly your *fault*." Brody pulled her hands, tugging her up from the seat. "People get sick, babe. It happens. The doc's right. Let's get some air."

"I should wait here," she resisted.

"For what?" Brody's voice was soft. Reasonable. His head dropped closer to hers. "Even if Hewitt and Sophia were here, they'd need to eat. They'd have to wait until the doctor cleared Eva for seeing them."

He was right. Knowing it did little to make up for the guilt that swamped her.

"I can't do this," she whispered hoarsely. "I just can't."

She had only a glimpse of Brody's narrowed eyes as she tugged her hands free of his, and slid past him, intent on escaping the waiting room.

She made it out into the corridor before he closed his hands over her shoulders, halting her from behind. Her throat ached and her eyes burned deep down inside her head. "Let me go."

He made a sound she couldn't interpret, and pulled her back into the waiting room, pushing closed the door that had been standing open.

"What's this really about?"

She hugged her arms around herself, feeling chilled. "I'm just tired. And relieved."

His lips twisted. "In the past week, I've seen you in pretty much every state a person can achieve. *Every* state."

She flushed miserably. "This isn't the time to joke."

"Who's joking?" His serious expression told her that he certainly wasn't. "I'm tired and relieved, too, and whatever is nagging at you is more than that."

"Brody—"

"Just spit it out, Angeline."

"I just…I just can't bear to make another wrong decision. The last time I did—" She broke off, shaking her head. "The last time," she tried again, "a boy died."

Brody sighed. He ran his hands down her arms, circling her wrists, lifting her palms until he could slide his fingers between hers. "You're a paramedic, love. Not even you can save everyone."

"I know. But this time, I should have. Just like now. With Eva. I should have recognized earlier that she was really ill! Instead, I was…you and I were…" She slid her hands free of his and raked back her hair. "We're supposed to be *protecting* Eva and Davey." She wasn't supposed to be falling in love with a completely unsuitable man.

"You think Eva's appendix would have been just dandy if she'd been with her parents, or with another bodyguard? Dream on, Angeline. Sometimes the best-laid plans get shot to hell, particularly when there are kids involved. But even if she were nineteen instead of nine, she could have gotten sick like this. There's no telling, and there's sure in hell no blaming."

"*You* would have noticed," she said thickly.

His eyebrows shot up. "Did you see me yanking her to a doctor any more quickly than we did?" He lowered his voice. "Tell me what happened with the boy."

"There's nothing to tell." She felt brittle. "He was only a kid. A gang member, they told me. And there was a shooting. I thought I could reach him from the rear side where the culvert wasn't so narrow." She swallowed. "I was wrong. By the time my partner and I reached him from the front side, the side *I* should have used in the first place, he'd bled out."

"And now you don't like going through tunnels," he murmured.

"I've *never* liked tunnels," she corrected. "Caves. None of that kind of thing."

"Caves." He let out a sigh. "I read in your file that you were hidden in one when Santo Marguerite was attacked."

She pressed her lips together, disconcerted that she had a file, much less one that he'd read. "The cave wasn't much for size. I was always told to stay out of it. But then someone—a cousin, maybe, because I don't remember my mother doing it—pushed me down into it." Not quickly enough for her to miss the attack on the village, though. "Davey's four," she murmured. "The same age I was when it happened. You suppose he's going to remember the madness we've put those children through these past few days?"

"If he does, his parents will help him deal

with it, just like Maggie and Daniel helped *you*."

"That boy still died, Brody. Because I hesitated. Because I knew if I went in that culvert, I'd freeze up."

"But you *did* go in the culvert."

"Too late."

"What about your partner?"

"He was a rookie. He was following my lead."

"So you were human and something went wrong. Are you going to keep beating yourself with it or are you going to pull it together and keep on keeping on? Angeline, I swear I have yet to see you hesitate even when I think you should. You see something that needs doing, and God. You do it. If you'd gotten to the kid any faster than you had would he have lived?"

She swallowed. Pressed her palms together. Shook her head. "Probably not." That's what her supervisor had said. That's what the emergency room doctors had said. "That's the only reason I have a job to go back to when my vacation is up." She waited a long beat, and finally admitted the truth. "If I go back at all. I just...I want to come back to Wyoming. I just don't want to come back feeling like I failed."

"You can't stop helping people, Angeline. You're a natural at it. So who the hell cares if you're doing it in Atlanta or in Weaver. Or Venezuela, or Sheridan for that matter?"

She jerked a little at that. "I put my fear ahead of my job, Brody, and that kid never had a chance. Today, with Eva, I put my…my need ahead of her." She waved her hand, encompassing the hospital waiting room around them. "And look where we are!"

"You made me feel human again," he said quietly. "You knew Eva and Davey were fed and bedded because *I* told you they were. So if you want to blame anyone, babe, it had better be me. Not yourself. You're a paramedic, for God's sake. Not a doctor. You're trained to respond to emergencies, which you've done pretty damn well as far as I'm concerned."

Her throat tightened. "But if I don't go back to Atlanta—"

"—then you don't go back," he said simply. He slid his hand through her hair. "The world's not gonna stop spinning, love, if you change courses. But that guilt?" He looked regretful. "Even when it's deserved, it doesn't do anything but dry a person up from the inside out. Let it go, Angeline."

"What do *you* know about guilt? You've probably never made a misstep in your entire life."

He slowly picked up her hand. The one with Sophia's wedding band. "I know that if I had kept quiet when I learned that Simon Brody wasn't my real father, he and my mother and Penny would all probably still be alive. Instead," he broke off and looked grim. "Instead, word got out to the wrong person that the man who *was* my real father had two kids and an ex-wife whose existence he'd managed to keep hidden for fifteen years. My mother broke the silence between them because of *me*. Because I wanted to know the man who'd really fathered me and Penny. And just like Santina would use Davey and Eva to manipulate their parents if they could, Sandoval tried using my family to manipulate *him*."

Shock swirled through her, thick and engulfing. "Oh, Brody. No. I'm so sorry. Sandoval? The same monster who destroyed Santo Marguerite? London's a far cry from Central and South America. Those were his stomping grounds, I thought. Why would he have reason to go after *your* family?"

"London had nothing to do with anything except that's where we lived. On the other hand, my father, the one who contributed his genes to me that is, was the one person who kept thwarting Sandoval's actions *wherever* they occurred," he said flatly. "And that's why my parents and sister died in a car bombing one fine spring afternoon. It was a total fluke that I wasn't with them."

Her stomach dropped. She stared at Brody's lips, waiting for him to continue.

But the door to the waiting room burst open and a tall, silver-haired man stood there, looking almost as surprised at the sight of *them*. But it wasn't surprise in his deep voice, when he spoke. It was annoyance. Pure and simple. "*There* you are. Bloody hell, Simon. You don't make it easy to find you, do you."

Brody's expression had grown, if anything, even more grim. His lips twisted. "I don't believe you've ever officially met," he told her, startling her out of her surprised stupor. "So let me have the honors. Angeline," he angled his head toward the older man, "meet Coleman Black."

Her stomach dropped to her toes, knowing what was coming even before Brody finished speaking.

"My father."

Chapter Fifteen

Brody watched the color drain from Angeline's face as she looked from him to Cole and back again. Her lips moved, as if she were struggling to find something appropriate to say, which only made Brody feel more like the slug he was for tossing her without preparation into the sordidness that was his life.

Cole gave him an annoyed look and crossed the room, his hand outstretched toward Angeline. "Simon isn't *quite* correct," he said smoothly. "We have met. But you were so small you wouldn't remember." He caught her hand in his, raising it to his lips. "You're as lovely as I would have expected, my dear."

Angeline looked disarmed, color coming back into her cheeks. Cole might be finally pushing retirement but that didn't mean the old man didn't have his charms.

As a father, however, he'd been pretty damn miserable.

"You saw me when I was a child?"

"All long hair and enormous brown eyes with barely a word of English to your name," he assured. "And now, you and my son here have been leading us all around in a merry chase. Needless to say, it was quite a surprise to actually have him call me for assistance." His gaze cut from Angeline to Brody, and there was no charm in the look for him.

It was pure steel.

Of course, the old man wouldn't be pleased that Brody had contacted him. It was entirely outside of protocol.

Brody deliberately smiled. He might be closing the gap to forty by leaps and bounds, but he still knew how to goad the guy, just as he had when he wasn't yet sixteen and Cole had pretty much dragged him, kicking and sullen, from London and taken him back with him to Connecticut.

He'd never sent out announcements that his son had come to live with him, that's for damn sure. Not hard when Brody hadn't actually lived *with* Cole. He'd been in a well-secured house, tended by well-trained agents, none of whom knew the entire story.

Nobody, not a single soul inside or outside of Hollins-Winword knew that Brody Paine was anything other than one more survivor taken under the protective wing of the agency until the suspected terrorist who'd targeted his family could be caught.

Which they never were, since Sandoval was still out there.

To this day, he didn't know if Cole had ever grieved over the loss of the woman he'd been married to for so brief a time. Or his daughter.

He'd never said.

And Brody sure in hell had never asked.

What they did do was exist in a sort of vacuum where Brody did his job and Cole did his, and rarely the twain ever met.

"Brody called you?" Angeline was looking at him with surprise. "He didn't tell me that."

"I told you I reached someone," he defended.

Her lips compressed.

"If you'd shown a lot less stubbornness and more sense," Cole told him, "you would have contacted me the first time you couldn't reach Persia, protocol be damned."

"Persia!" Angeline gave them both a horrified look. "That…that, *girl* who replaced me at the All-Med site is your handler?"

"Was," Cole said. "She's been…replaced."

"But why?"

"Don't bother asking, babe. He doesn't answer questions like that."

"Miguel Chavez discovered she was playing both ends from the middle when she made a few unwise calls while returning that Hummer to St. Agnes. Hewitt was the one who donated that to the nuns, by the way."

Brody felt sure that Cole wouldn't have provided the information about Persia if not for the pleasure of proving him wrong. And he didn't much like that the old man had shown the same curiosity he'd felt about the presence of that expensive truck at the convent in the first place.

"Miguel." Angeline looked dazed. She sat down on the nearest chair. "*He* is involved with Hollins, too?"

"On occasion," Cole said briefly. "As he got to know you through your volunteer work with All-Med he thought you might be a good asset, and that's when I sent Brody to meet you there five years ago."

She shook her head. "Most people would just pick up the phone and set a meeting," she murmured.

Cole laughed.

"Sweet as this reunion is," Brody drawled, "why didn't someone replace Persia sooner?"

His father's laughter died. He looked irritated all over again. "We didn't know where the hell you were. The only trace we found of either of you was an All-Med T-shirt covered in blood on the floor of a cab that was riddled with your fingerprints in Caracas. That's when we were positive it was the two of you, and not Santina's man, who managed to get the Stanley children out of St. Agnes. Until then, we had no confirmation either way. You can imagine the difficulties that has presented."

"Good grief," Angeline hopped back to her feet. "My family doesn't know about the shirt, do they?"

"Unfortunately, yes. The media down there

got wind of an aid volunteer seeming to disappear off the planet, with nothing left behind but her bloody shirt. Damn reporters. Always messing things around when they shouldn't. If you'd ever turn on a television and watch the international news, Simon, you might know these things."

Angeline groaned. Any television viewing for them of late had been geared toward Davey's four-year-old tastes.

"But I've let your folks know that you're safe," Cole assured. "I notified them earlier as soon as I heard from Simon."

She pressed her hand to her forehead. "They must have been going mad." She eyed them both. "This is *exactly* why I didn't want them knowing I was involved with Hollins. We're all worried enough about my cousin who's still missing!"

Cole stayed silent on that and Brody wanted to kick him. But the fact was, Ryan Clay *was* missing. Not even the agency had been able to unearth him, and they'd been quietly trying for months. That news wasn't likely to make any one of them feel better.

"Your parents will see for themselves soon enough that you're safe and well," Cole warned. "Daniel told me he and Maggie would be here by morning."

Angeline's hands flopped down to her sides. "Well, great. I never mind seeing my parents. I, um, I have to go check on Eva. I don't suppose in all these revelations you can tell me that her parents are free?"

"I wish I could," Cole told her. "We're working on it," he added. "We know where they're being held in Rio, and that they're very much alive. Getting them out, however, has been proving problematic."

From experience, Brody knew that term could mean just about anything.

"I'll go with you to see Eva," he told her and ignored the eyebrow his father lifted in surprise.

Angeline nodded, moistened her lips and turned toward Cole. "It's been an…eventful night, I must say." She leaned up and pressed a kiss to his cheek. "Thank you. For everything that you've done for me. For my family. It's nice to have an opportunity to tell you that, in person, after all these years."

He smiled faintly. "I like to see a happy ending as much as anyone. That's what keeps me in this business. Sadly, the people closest to me weren't able to find that." His gaze cut to Brody's, and for once, he let his regret show. "But now I have hope again."

Brody didn't even want to know what that was supposed to mean.

He closed his hand around Angeline's elbow and drew her toward the door. Eva would surely be settled in her room by now.

"Simon. A word, please."

He should have known. Cole always had liked to have the last word.

"Stay," Angeline murmured. "Talk with him. Come to Eva's room when you're finished." She looked around him. "Mr. Black, I hope we see one another again."

"Coleman. Or Cole, if you choose." He looked slightly amused. "And I feel certain that we will."

Brody waited until she'd disappeared down the hall and around the corner before he looked back at his father. *"What?"*

"Are you willing to stay on the Stanley children until that situation is resolved? I've already arranged for a team to keep watch over the hospital, either way."

Brody's lips thinned. When had he ever let go of an op before it was completed? "Do you need to ask?"

"I suppose not. You're good at what you do, Simon. Too good when it comes down to it."

"Is there a point in there somewhere? Because I'd kind of like to see how Eva's doing after they've cut her open."

Cole's lips compressed. "Touché," he said evenly. "I was never there when you were in the hospital being patched up from your various escapades. Of which there were *many.* So maybe my point is moot, after all."

He didn't want to care what the man had to say. But he did. For the same reasons that he'd gone back to the agency even after he'd planned to hang out his shingle with Roger.

He *was* like Cole.

Dammit all to hell.

So he stood there. Waiting. "Well?"

"Don't turn into me," Cole said simply. "If Angeline matters to you, and it seems that she does, change your ways and make a life with her. Hang out that law degree you worked so hard to get. Do anything but this. You can't combine being a field agent with a family."

"Tristan Clay did." Hell, Angeline's uncle was pretty high up the Hollins food chain of command.

Cole's expression didn't change. "I could easily name fifty other agents who have not. So what odds would you lay your money on? Whether you want to admit it or not, Simon, you're too much like me. I'm just suggesting you not make the same choices that I did. The cost is too high. You're old enough to recognize what matters in life, and young enough still to do something about it."

"Don't pretend that you know me all that well, Cole. We both know otherwise."

The other man pulled out a pipe, looked around the waiting room that was clearly marked "no smoking" and tucked it away again. "I know enough to recognize the ring that Angeline is wearing."

"It was my mother's first wedding ring from Simon," Brody said tightly. Before she'd been buried, he'd taken it from her favorite jewelry box, the one where she'd kept her dearest possessions. "It has nothing to do with you."

"Did she tell you that?"

"Yes." He bit out the word.

Cole smiled, but there was no happiness in it. Only years of weariness and a sadness that seemed to go a mile deep. "Actually," he said quietly, "it was the ring that *I* gave her."

Then he turned and walked out of the waiting room.

When Angeline found the room the nurse directed her to, Eva was sound asleep.

She sat down beside the bed and rested her hands lightly on the mattress.

The ring on her finger winked up at her.

She toyed with it. Slipped it off easily, for it *was* loose. Yet, in all the madness of the past several days, she'd managed to keep it in place.

"You kept wearing it."

She looked up to see Brody standing in the doorway. "You kept telling people we were married," she pointed out truthfully enough.

His gaze slanted toward the bed, as if he'd already lost interest in the subject. "How's she doing?"

"Sound asleep, as you can see." She curled her fingers, wanting to hide the ring from his too-seeing eyes. "How are *you* doing?"

He exhaled. "Does it matter?"

She pushed back the chair and rose. "Of course it matters, Brody."

"How much?"

She wavered. "What do you want me to say? I don't know what you're asking."

His eyes were nearly black. "I think you know."

Her spine stiffened. Did he want her to lay her soul bare merely for pure entertainment value? "Just what did you and your father talk about?"

"How much like him I am."

"Don't make that sound like such a death sentence," she chided softly. "I know you have your reasons for feeling differently, *good* reasons, but if it weren't for him…" She lifted her shoulders. What more could she say?

"Santo Marguerite might still be standing if Hollins-Winword hadn't tried to intervene."

"You mean if your father hadn't tried." She sighed. "Sandoval is the monster in this story, Brody. Not your— not Coleman Black."

She could see the resistance in his eyes and stepped closer, folding her hands around his. "It wasn't anyone but Sandoval who wanted the land around my family's village. The likelihood that he'd have done something terrible regardless of your father's presence there—of any kind of Hollins-Winword involvement for that matter—is extremely high. If it didn't happen when I was four, it could have happened before I was born, or twenty years after. Am I right? *Am I?*"

"He's still active, obviously," he allowed grimly.

"Exactly. And Sandoval still controls that land, even to this day. My father told me long ago that there's no reasoning with a man like him. My surviving what happened there makes no more sense than you not being in the car that day with your family. We survived. They didn't. That's reality and you and I get to live with it. And maybe," she swallowed, "maybe it's time we stop questioning why, and just accept the blessing for what it is. Your father—I'm sorry—*Coleman* helped me to a new life as a Clay. And I'm assuming he played some role in your life after your parents and sister died?"

"Only enough to make sure nobody else got wind of who I really was. He put a roof over my head in Connecticut and guards on my tail and the only thing we ever talked about was the agency."

"Why would he do that? Because you think he didn't care? Don't you think it might be because he didn't want to lose you, too? It's your past, Brody. You know it better than I, obviously. But regardless of how or why anything happened with your childhood or with mine, here we are. Survivors." She looked over at the bed. "Did he say anything more about them?"

"Just made sure I wasn't going to bail on the situation."

"He wouldn't think that."

He snorted softly. "Like you said once. We're going to have to agree to disagree where Coleman Black is concerned. You don't have to worry about any Santina folks showing up here, though. He told me there's a team watching the hospital now."

"If *he* and all of Hollins-Winword that he has at his command weren't able to track us here until you contacted him, I don't think Santina would be able to find us, either. But now that everything's out in the open, more or less, I guess there's no more need for me to be here. Or, like you said, for this." She slipped off the ring and held it out to him, wanting with everything she possessed for him to tell her that she was wrong.

To tell her that *she* mattered.

That he wanted her to stay for reasons that had nothing to do with Eva or Davey or anything but what had gone between them.

He slowly lifted his palm.

It was not the answer she wanted.

She sucked down the pain inside her, and prayed that it didn't show on her face.

No woman wanted to face the fact that the man she'd fallen in love with didn't return the feeling.

Without touching him, she dropped the ring into his palm.

His fingers slowly curled around it. "The ring wasn't what I thought it was," he murmured.

"It wasn't what I thought, either." Despite herself, the words emerged. She pressed her lips together, keeping her composure together with an effort.

She turned to the bed, wrapping her hands around the iron rail at the foot of it. "So, um, what now? I still h-have a week of vacation left. I'd like to spend it with, um, with Davey and Eva. If you don't mind." Her eyes burned and she blinked furiously, determined not to cry in front of him.

"And after your week is up?"

"Then I'll go back h-home." In all of the time they'd spent together, he'd never before been cruel like this.

"In Atlanta?"

"What do you want from me, Brody? Maybe I'll stay in Atlanta. Maybe I'll go back to Weaver. *I don't know.*"

"Is there anything that you *do* know?"

Stung, she slapped her hands on the rail. Eva didn't so much as stir. "I know I must have been a fool to let myself love you," she snapped. "So if you want to know how much you matter, *now* you do. Are you quite satisfied?"

"I don't know. I haven't been loved in a long time." His voice sounded rusty. "I'm out of practice."

And just that simply, her anger eased out of her, leaving nothing but her heart that ached for him.

"I think you've been loved all along, you just haven't wanted to face it."

"I don't want to talk about Cole."

She angled her chin, looking up at him. "Then who do you want to talk about?"

"You. Me." His blue eyes were steady on her face. "It's been a crazy week."

"It hasn't even been a week," she whispered, feeling choked.

"But it's been years of foreplay."

She flushed and opened her mouth. Caught the faint smile playing around his lips and closed it again.

"I love you, Angeline Reyes Clay. I know that seems fast, but it's been a long time in the making. And maybe I'm not so far gone that I can't heed good advice when I hear it even if I don't care much for the person delivering it. Maybe I'm just tired of making my way alone. Or maybe the fact that we both survived, like you said, meant we were supposed to find our way here to each other. But what I do know is that I don't want you to walk away from me when your vacation is done. Fact is, I don't want you to walk away from me ever."

A tear slid down her cheek. "Brody."

"I don't want you to go back to Atlanta unless that's really where you want to be. And then, hell, I don't know. I guess I'd follow you there. But then I'd have to drag you back here, because, *babe*. A city? When we've got all of Wyoming at our disposal? If you don't like the house I built, I'll build you another. A dozen if I have to. One thing I can say about Hollins is that it does pay well. I could even start a law practice. But if I didn't, I can still support you. And, you know. Kids. If you wanted."

She laughed, the tears coming faster. "You'd want kids? *You?* Not long ago you shuddered at the idea!"

"I'm a guy," he dismissed. "Don't you think I'd be good at it?"

She tilted her head, tsking. "Brody."

"So?" He looked oddly unsure of himself.

"You're really serious," she breathed, hardly daring to believe that he didn't want just the here and now. He wanted…more.

"I'm a serious man," he said gruffly, pulling her into his arms. "In the serious business of loving you." He held up his hand and she saw the ring tucked on the end of his index finger. "This was my mother's," he said. "I thought it was the ring my dad— Simon—gave her. She treasured it," he murmured. "But it was from Cole."

"Why didn't you say something before? I thought you'd gotten it from the Stanleys' apartment."

"It was easier to let you think that than let

you know that, even then, you mattered to me." His hand shook a little as he drew it down her cheek, and she leaned into his touch, the tears sliding down her cheek.

"I love you, Brody. And I don't want to go anywhere that you're not."

"I'll get you your own ring," he said huskily.

She pressed her lips to his for a long, long moment. Then she drew his hand with the ring to her, clasping it against her heart. "Do you think that Coleman didn't love your mother when he gave this to her?"

A shadow came and went in his eyes. "I don't know anymore."

"I think he did," she whispered. "And you know she treasured it, because you said so. So maybe this *is* the ring I'm meant to have, Brody. Maybe we're all just finally coming full circle. Like the ring itself. No beginning. No end."

"If you want this ring, just say so, Angeline." But the sudden sheen in his eyes gave lie to his wry words, and her heart slipped open even more to him.

This utterly *good* man in his heart, who was a positive whirlwind. Who shocked her and delighted her, who challenged her and had faith in her, even when she didn't have it in herself.

"I want your ring, Brody Paine," she whispered surely. "And even if there were no ring at all, I'd still want you. I'd still love you."

"You think this has been a crazy few days? Be sure, Angeline. Because I won't let you go."

She slid her hand up his chest, over the bunch of bandage she could feel beneath, until she found his heartbeat, pulsing against her palm. "What's a few crazy days when we've got a lifetime of them yet to live?"

His head came down to hers. "Together." The word whispered over her lips.

She closed the distance, her heart as full as it could possibly ever be. "Together."

Epilogue

"Where are the boutonnieres?" Casey Clay sauntered into the room where the groom's half of the wedding party was assembling before the wedding.

"Davey's guarding them on the counter there." Brody pointed to the boy, who wore a miniature black suit like his. Davey, looking important, handed over the sprig when Casey went to him.

Stephanotis or some such thing, Brody knew. He'd been hearing about flowers for the past month. Ever since his and Angeline's plans for a simple elopement flew right out the window.

She hadn't wanted to disappoint her family, she'd told him. And he'd caved rather than see any disappointment darken her eyes. He figured she deserved the wedding of her dreams. It was the least he could do to make up for proposing in a damn hospital room after five of the most insane days of their lives.

Now, he stared at himself in the mirror, trying to get the knot in his damned tie straight. Thank God he had insisted on no bow ties.

As it was, the wedding that he'd figured he could slide Angeline quickly through had turned into a regular circus. They couldn't hold it at the house in Sheridan, because the entire family was in Weaver. Angeline had been raised in the church there, so of course she ought to be married there.

On and on and on.

"How're you holding up?" Max Scalise held out a tall glass of champagne. Brody took it, though he'd have preferred a beer.

"Fine, if I could get this bloody tie straight."

"Just think about the honeymoon," Max advised, thoroughly amused. He reached over and yanked the long silver tie front and center. "You look real pretty."

"Don't make me regret asking you to be my best man," he muttered, polishing off the champagne all too quickly. Roger had sent his regrets that he couldn't make the wedding, so the position had needed filling. And now that Max was the sheriff and married to Sarah, he evidently no longer had reason to loathe the ground that Brody walked. Brody had even begun to actually like the other guy. He was a good cop.

"Don't make me regret agreeing," the other man returned. "What're you so grouchy about? You've got a beautiful woman, and I mean *seriously* beautiful, ready to commit the rest of her life to you. Most folks would just think she needed committing."

"Hilarious."

"This is just a day, Brody. It's the marriage that counts."

"I know. Believe me. I know. It's just all this…" he waved his hand at the flowers, the champagne. "Never in my life did I figure I'd ever be doing this."

"Did you ever figure you'd have someone like Angeline in your life?"

"No." He turned back to the mirror. Started to reach for the tie only to decide it looked fine the way it was. "She's been staying in Weaver for the past week," he finally said under his breath. While he'd been in Sheridan with Davey and Eva and Mrs. B. making plans to open that law practice. Finally. "We're going bloody insane without her. What's it going to be like ten years down the road and she wants to go away for a week or something?"

"God. You do have it bad." Max clapped him over the shoulder. "Suck it up," he advised, obviously amused. "Be a man."

From the sanctuary, Brody heard the organ music begin playing.

"Here." Casey held out the boutonniere. He, like Evan Taggart and young Davey, was serving as Brody's groomsmen. "Don't want to forget your posies."

Brody managed to pin the thing into place without stabbing himself to death and then, just as they'd rehearsed the evening before, they filed into the church.

His eyes drifted over the guests. No "his" and "her" sides, Angeline had said. Because everything from here on out was an "our" situation.

Mostly, he figured, she knew his side would be pretty damn empty otherwise, and soft heart that she had, she thought that would bother him.

He watched Casey escort his mother, Maggie, up the aisle where orchids dripped from the sides of each pew. Her blond hair was twisted in a sleek knot, her slender figure accentuated by the dark blue dress she wore. Next to her hulking son Casey—who'd definitely inherited the tall-blond-Clay thing— she looked even more petite.

Her eyes met Brody's and she smiled as she took her seat in the front pew. Once she'd taken him to task for dragging his daughter around the world and scaring the life out of them the way he had, she'd welcomed him with more generosity than he deserved.

Clearly, Angeline took after her.

Sitting behind Maggie were Angeline's grandparents, Squire and Gloria. And behind *them,* the rows on both sides of the church were jammed with more relatives. Angeline had counted them off for him one day and the number had been staggering, particularly for a guy who had only his quasi father to claim.

He was sitting in the front row on Brody's nonside.

Again, Angeline's doing. She'd insisted he invite Cole. Brody hadn't believed the man would even show up, but there he was. Just another surprise in his life since Angeline.

The organ music changed suddenly and everyone turned expectantly toward the rear of the church.

Brody realized he was holding his breath.

Sarah came first, and beside him, he heard Max sigh a little at the sight of his wife, who was noticeably pregnant in her long blue dress. And Max had said that Brody had it bad? He shot his best man a look. Max just shrugged. He was thoroughly besotted and didn't care who knew it.

Close on Sarah's heels was Leandra. As small as Sarah was tall, she came up the aisle, not seeming to look at anyone but her husband, Evan.

"She's pregnant," Max murmured to Brody. "Just told him before they got to the church."

Which would explain the vaguely dazed look on the vet's face, Brody suspected, and felt a definite envy. He'd told Angeline just a week ago that he wasn't getting any younger; they needed to get cracking.

Of course, at the time, he'd mostly just wanted to get her into bed, but she'd blushed and looked so suddenly shy that he hadn't been able to get the hope out of his head.

Davey and Eva headed up the aisle. The boy held a pillow with the rings tied to it in ribbon, and it was a good thing because he kept tipping the pillow back and forth as he grinned widely, happy to be the center of attention. And Eva— fully recuperated in the past six weeks since her appendectomy—looked pretty as a picture with her hair up in curls, wearing the same blue as the women. She had a smile on her face, too, and Brody was glad to see it, since Hewitt and Sophia's absence had been hitting her harder than Davey.

He gave Eva a subtle wink and she wrinkled her nose, smiling wider. Lord, but he was going to miss them. He, the guy who had always preached never getting too attached.

J.D. was sauntering up the aisle, and Brody's mouth dried a little, because he knew Angeline came after her. As if she could read his mind, J.D.'s green gaze was full of laughter as she passed him, and took her place in line. She gave him an audacious wink. Since she'd given Brody the third degree at the rehearsal the night before, evidently she'd decided she could be sparing with her good humor now.

He grinned back at her. Yeah, he liked J.D. She was a good kid.

And then he saw her. The only woman he'd ever loved.

Angeline.

Standing in the rear of the church looking so beautiful he thought his heart might lurch out of his throat.

The afternoon sun slanted through the high windows above their heads, as the organ swelled and she slowly started forward, her hand on her father's arm. She'd told him she wasn't going to wear white, but the long dress she wore looked pretty white to him. The soft-looking lace clung to her figure, looking innocent and sexy all at once.

Her long dark hair was pulled back from her face, only a single, exotic flower tucked in the gleaming waves, and when she finally reached him, she angled a look up at him. She slowly, softly smiled. "You ready for a wedding, Brody Paine?"

As long as she kept smiling at him, there was nothing in life that he couldn't face, he thought. Even a wedding in Wyoming.

"Only with you," he promised and knew he'd do the whole thing a dozen times over, just to see the shining in her eyes.

She tucked her hand surely in his, and handed off her bouquet of orchids to J.D., and the two of them stepped up into the chancel with the minister, who beamed a smile over all of them and opened his bible.

"Dearly beloved," he began, only to be interrupted when Davey suddenly bolted for the rear of the church.

"Mom! Dad!" His voice filled the rafters. Eva suddenly dropped her bouquet and pelted after him.

Angeline's startled eyes met Brody's and they all turned.

Sophia and Hewitt Stanley were rushing up the aisle, grabbing their kids up and swinging them around.

Angeline bit her lip. She looked up at Brody, who didn't look as surprised as everyone else. Nor did Coleman, when she gave him an inquiring look.

He smiled. Lifted his hands.

In their pew, Angeline's parents were holding hands and looking amused. After all, twenty-five years earlier, Angeline's arrival had very nearly interrupted *their* nuptials.

"I suppose you knew they were coming," Angeline whispered to Brody.

"I wasn't sure when they would get here. They were extracted two days ago," he told her. "There was a lot of debriefing. At least a few of the Santina group are going to be out of commission for a long while."

"And Sandoval?"

He shook his head. "Not everything can be solved, sometimes."

Davey was dragging his parents by their hands toward them. "Mr. Dad, this is my *real* dad."

Both Hewitt and his wife were pale from their ordeal, but the hand he extended was steady. "Thank you," he said simply.

Sophia's eyes were wet. She held Eva tight against her.

Angeline crouched down and touched the girl's cheek. "I told you faith could do amazing things." She felt Brody's hand squeeze her shoulder.

Eva's face was wet with tears as she

twisted an arm around Angeline's neck, too. "I love you, Angeline."

"I love you, too, sweetie. And I'm going to miss you, but we'll see each other again." Her eyes blurred with the promise as she rose and faced Sophia. "I feel like I know you."

"And I feel like we will never have truer friends," Sophia returned, looking just as tearful as her daughter. She hugged Angeline tightly. "But we are interrupting. We would have waited outside if we'd realized the ceremony had already begun. But there was a message from a Mrs. Bedford that the children were *here*."

"Of course you had to come. Right away," Angeline assured. She brushed her hand down her antique gown. "So now you'll stay…find a seat," she suggested, laughing.

Coleman gestured, and the four of them joined him in that front pew. He rescued the pillow with the rings that Davey had dropped on the floor. His gaze hesitated for a moment on the smaller of the two bands. Then he handed it to Brody. "You'll be happy," he told him gruffly.

"I know," Brody replied simply. He took

the pillow and handed it off to Max. Then he turned to Angeline. "Shall we try this again?"

She dashed her fingers over her cheeks and nodded. She folded her hand through his arm again, and they stepped up into the chancel where the minister was looking slightly bewildered. He opened his bible once again.

"House is going to feel empty without them," Brody murmured before the man could begin speaking.

Angeline huffed out a puff of air. "You know, don't you. Are you going to *ever* let me surprise you?"

He gave a bark of laughter and caught her around her waist, lifting her right off her toes. "Brody," she gasped, but she was smiling and looped her arms around his shoulders.

"Every day with you is a surprise, Angeline," he told her and kissed her deeply. The guests were laughing. Some cheering. She barely heard any of it.

Oh, she loved this man who loved her.

The minister cleared his throat. Loudly. "If we could have a little order, here?"

Brody set Angeline on her feet again. He reached out and opened the bible for the minister, pointing at the pages. "Right there," he said.

The minister's lips thinned. But there was a definite twinkle in his eyes that even *he* couldn't hide. "Never a dull moment when there's a Clay around," he murmured. "All right then." He lifted the bible higher. Looked at Angeline and Brody, then at the congregation behind them. "Dearly beloved…"

* * * * *

THE ROYAL HOUSE OF NIROLI
Always passionate, always proud

The richest royal family in the world—
united by blood and passion,
torn apart by deceit and desire

Nestled in the azure blue of the Mediterranean Sea, the majestic island of Niroli has prospered for centuries. The Fierezza men have worn the crown with passion and pride since ancient times. But now, as the king's health declines, and his two sons have been tragically killed, the crown is in jeopardy.

The clock is ticking—a new heir must be found before the king is forced to abdicate. By royal decree the internationally scattered members of the Fierezza family are summoned to claim their destiny. But any person who takes the throne must do so according to The Rules of the Royal House of Niroli. Soon secrets and rivalries emerge as the descendents of this ancient royal line vie for position and power. Only a true Fierezza can become ruler—a person dedicated to their country, their people…and their eternal love!

Each month starting in July 2007,
Harlequin Presents is delighted to bring you
an exciting installment from
THE ROYAL HOUSE OF NIROLI,
in which you can follow the epic search
for the true Nirolian king.
Eight heirs, eight romances, eight fantastic stories!

Here's your chance to enjoy a sneak preview of the first book delivered to you by royal decree…

FIVE minutes later she was standing immobile in front of the study's window, her original purpose of coming in forgotten, as she stared in shocked horror at the envelope she was holding. Waves of heat followed by icy chill surged through her body. She could hardly see the address now through her blurred vision, but the crest on its left-hand front corner stood out, its *royal* crest, followed by the address: *HRH Prince Marco of Niroli...*

She didn't hear Marco's key in the apartment door, she didn't even hear him calling out her name. Her shock was so great that nothing could penetrate it. It encased her in a kind of bubble, which only concentrated the torment of what she was suffering and branded it on her brain so that it could never be forgotten. It was only finally pierced by the sudden opening of the study door as Marco walked in.

"Welcome home, *Your Highness*. I suppose I ought to curtsy." She waited, praying that he would laugh and tell her that she had got it all wrong, that the envelope she was holding, addressing him as Prince Marco of Niroli, was some silly mistake. But like a tiny candle flame shivering vulnerably in the dark, her hope trembled fearfully. And then the look in Marco's eyes extinguished it as cruelly as a hand placed callously over a dying person's face to stem their last breath.

"Give that to me," he demanded, taking the envelope from her.

"It's too late, Marco," Emily told him brokenly. "I know the truth now…." She dug her teeth in her lower lip to try to force back her own pain.

"You had no right to go through my desk," Marco shot back at her furiously, full of loathing at being caught off guard and forced into a position in which he was in the wrong, making him determined to find something he could accuse Emily of. "I trusted you...."

Emily could hardly believe what she was hearing. "No, you didn't trust me, Marco, and you didn't trust me because you knew that I couldn't trust you. And you knew that because you're a liar, and liars don't trust people because they know that they themselves cannot be trusted." She not only felt sick, she also felt as though she could hardly breathe. "You are Prince Marco of Niroli.... How could you not tell me who you are and still live with me as intimately as we have lived together?" she demanded brokenly.

"Stop being so ridiculously dramatic," Marco demanded fiercely. "You are making too much of the situation."

"*Too much?*" Emily almost screamed the words at him. "When were you going to tell me, Marco? Perhaps you just planned to walk away without telling me anything? After all, what do my feelings matter to you?"

"Of course they matter." Marco stopped her sharply. "And it was in part to protect them, and you, that I decided not to inform you when my grandfather first announced that he intended to step down from the throne and hand it on to me."

"To protect me?" Emily nearly choked on her fury. "Hand on the throne? No wonder you told me when you first took me to bed that all you wanted was sex. You *knew* that was the only kind of relationship there could ever be between us! You *knew* that one day you would be Niroli's king. No doubt you are expected to marry a princess. Is she picked out for you already, your *royal* bride?"

* * * * *

Look for
THE FUTURE KING'S PREGNANT MISTRESS
by Penny Jordan in July 2007,
from Harlequin Presents,
available wherever books are sold.

SPECIAL EDITION™

Emotional, compelling stories that capture the intensity of living, loving and creating a family in today's world.

Desire

Modern, passionate reads that are powerful and provocative.

nocturne

Dramatic and sensual tales of paranormal romance.

Romantic SUSPENSE

Romances that are sparked by danger and fueled by passion.

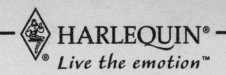

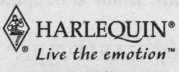

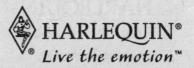

HARLEQUIN®
INTRIGUE®

BREATHTAKING ROMANTIC SUSPENSE

Shared dangers and passions lead to electrifying
romance and heart-stopping suspense!

Every month, you'll meet six new heroes
who are guaranteed to make your spine tingle
and your pulse pound. With them you'll enter
into the exciting world of Harlequin Intrigue—
where your life is on the line
and so is your heart!

THAT'S INTRIGUE—
ROMANTIC SUSPENSE
AT ITS BEST!

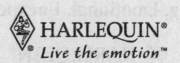

HARLEQUIN®
Live the emotion™

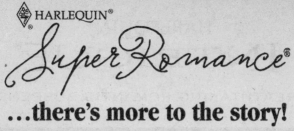
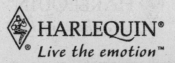